To Brodie, C. J.

Proverbs 3:5–6

Warm thanks to:
My husband, Randy, for taking us to the Kilauea volcano in Hawaii.
Your love of travel and adventure has been a blessing on this journey.

Marie, David, and Andrew. You are an unending source of
inspiration and your encouragement is priceless.

Wayne and Phyllis Banman, Rachel Dyck, Ingrid Friesen,
Linda Janzen, Cindy Klassen, Marie Peters, Mary Poetker,
Sharon Toews, and Grace Warkentin.
Thank you for praying for this series. Your intercessions make
this possible.

Dr. Carl Duerksen for helping me get the medical details right.

Dr. Gus Konkel for guiding my understanding of
the fifth commandment.

Heather Gemmen, Carol Ann Hiemstra, and Lora Riley—this book is
so much better because of your editorial skills and creativity.

Dr. Alf Bell for your inspiring sermon
"God Bless Our Families" at Lakeside Baptist in Kenora, Ontario.

"Honor your father and your mother,
so that you may live long in the land
the LORD your God is giving you."

Exodus 20:12

— ONE —

THE TIME STONE

Joshua Donald MacKenzie! What in the world is going on?" Josh's mom thrust her hands onto her hips, lowered her eyebrows, and gave him a ferocious stare.

Josh froze, clutching his basketball against his chest and glanced over at his twin brother. Will stood a meter away on the driveway, looking confused.

"What did you do?" whispered Will.

"Um, nothing much."

Their mother stepped out of the house, closing the door behind her. Both boys took a step back.

"Judging by her expression, I'd say you did something," said Will. A small smile stole onto his face. He loved it when Josh got into trouble—especially when it didn't have anything to do with him.

"I … um …" Before Josh could finish, his mother strode toward them, arms pumping, until she reached the spot where the boys had been shooting hoops. Her eyes zeroed in on Josh like a laser beam seeking its target. He dropped the basketball and ducked behind Will, using his brother as a shield.

"Let go of me," screeched Will, trying to get out of the way and struggling to push his glasses back in place. "Mom, I don't know what Josh did, but whatever it is, it had nothing to do with me."

Josh wrapped his arms around Will's waist and pulled him backward. The two boys scurried crablike across the lawn; their mom stalked after them. They didn't stop until Josh's back connected with the lilac hedge that separated their yard from their neighbors'.

Their mom lunged forward and grabbed both boys by the arms. "I've got you now. Wait until your father hears about this."

"Hears about what?" whined Will.

"You had me fooled for a little while. You two are pretty clever. How many times have you pulled this little stunt before?"

"This was the first time, honest," whimpered Josh. "I really practiced up until today."

"Good. Then you'll have no trouble with your new practice schedule. We're doubling your time for the next four weeks. It'll be one hour a day, no matter what."

"That's not fair," groaned Josh. He gave her his best sad-puppy-dog face. "Come on, it was just a joke."

Her expression softened for a moment until Will interrupted again. "Would someone please tell me what's going on?"

Josh looked down at his feet, feeling partly guilty but mostly proud of himself. "It was my idea. Will didn't have anything to do with it. I used the tape recorder from my spy kit to tape him. He didn't have a clue."

Will frowned. "Taped me doing what?"

"Practicing your violin."

"Why?" Will looked really confused.

"I played a tape of you practicing when I was supposed to be practicing so I could come out here and play basketball with you."

Will's jaw dropped. "You did what?"

Josh managed to hold back a smile, but he couldn't hide the twinkle in his eyes. He was awfully pleased with himself but not sure if it was safe to show it. "You've got to admit, I'm pretty creative."

"You're creative, all right," agreed his mother, looking at Josh thoughtfully.

Josh grabbed her hand. "So how about we just pretend this never happened? I'll practice good from now on, I promise."

She sighed. "I'll let you off with double practice time just for today if you promise to never do that again. Do we have a deal?"

"But then I'm not going to have any time to do anything else. That's not fair," protested Josh.

She pulled her hand away and started walking back to the house. Josh and Will trailed behind her at a distance.

"You need to learn when to keep your big mouth shut," muttered Will. "She would have let you off easy."

Their mother was almost at the house when she stopped and turned around. "We'll go back to our first plan—you can double your violin practice time every day for the next four weeks."

Josh scampered up to her. "No, Mom ... really ... it's okay. I'll practice right now and get it over with."

She gave him a tight-lipped smile. "I meant that part about never doing that again, Josh. How on earth did you think you'd sneak that past me? You and Will don't even play the same songs. He's two grades ahead of you in violin. It's wrong to pretend you did something when you really didn't."

"I was hoping you'd think I'd really improved," he replied sheepishly.

Will came up from behind. "Mom's right. I don't know why you thought you could get away with that. You'll never play as well as I do. You don't practice enough."

Their mother gave Will a stern look. "That's enough, Will. This discussion's over."

He let out a little groan. "Yes, Mother."

She opened the door and gently pushed Josh inside the house. "Go tune your violin. I'll be there in five minutes to help you practice your scales."

"I have to practice with *you?*"

"Should we go up to triple time? We could add thirty minutes of nonstop scales to your practice."

Josh slumped to one side, using the doorframe to prop himself up. "I'll never survive a one-hour practice with you."

"Oh, yes, you will," replied his mom, planting a kiss on his cheek. "Go tune your violin. I'll see you in five minutes."

An hour later, Josh wandered upstairs to his bedroom, his arm aching from his vigorous practice. "Why do I have to play the stupid violin?" he grumbled to himself. "And who really cares if I play in tune or not?"

He pushed open his bedroom door, stopping for a minute to inspect the room he shared with his brother. It always amazed him how he and Will could be such complete opposites—and their bedroom was just one example. While Josh's clothes, both clean and dirty, were scattered on the floor along with some half-finished homework assignments and a few battered sports magazines, Will's clothes carefully hung in the closet. And if that wasn't bad enough, Will had arranged his reference books, textbooks, and binders in neat stacks on his desk.

I bet he's already finished his homework ... and now he's studying something "just for fun." Josh shook his head at the thought. *Good thing I have Ellen.*

Their older sister was much easier to get along with. He liked spending time with her. She was far braver than Will and liked to try new things, a real bonus on the time-travel missions they had been going on lately. Best of all, she always had time for him. Other than the fact that she was a girl, she was perfect.

Josh crossed the room, opened his underwear drawer, and felt around. He pulled out his compass, glanced at it, and looped its string around his neck. Reaching into the drawer a little further, he dug out the time stone from underneath a pile of mismatched socks. He curled his fingers around it, and startled by its cold, smooth surface, lifted it up to his cheek. After holding it there for a minute, he plopped down onto his bed, the stone securely in his hand. "Today would be a good day to go on a trip. Do you think you could turn on?"

Josh had discovered the time stone embedded in his front lawn months ago. He knew right away there was something special about it, but he hadn't realized how extraordinary it was until he woke up in the middle of the night and discovered the stone projecting pictures onto the wall, much like a tiny slide projector. Every minute or so, the picture changed. Josh had accidentally touched it when it was projecting a picture of a jungle onto the wall and a whirlwind appeared from out of nowhere and transported him and his siblings back in time. They landed in a Mayan jungle hundreds of years ago and helped a young girl escape from an evil shaman.

From that time on, every so often the stone turned on again, taking the three of them on an adventure. So far they'd traveled to a medieval castle in England, where they found a stolen jeweled cross; to an ancient laboratory in Prague, where they helped a kindly old alchemist with his experiments; and to a warring aboriginal village in Canada long before the time of the white man.

As far as Josh was concerned, the only disadvantage of his time stone was that he never knew when it was going to send them on another journey. Even though their adventures were terrifying at times, he loved going.

Josh gently lowered his hands onto his lap, the stone resting in the middle of his upturned palm. "I know we're not ready to go—Will thinks we should spend days packing before we go anywhere or do anything—but that doesn't matter. We've always done fine. We always managed to find everything we needed on our other adventures." He glanced down at the stone. "Come on, you can do it. Turn on so we can go again."

A jolt of electricity surged through his hand. He squealed and jumped up, dropping the stone onto his bed. It landed on the middle of his pillow. As he watched, it made a quiet whirring sound and a small round hole opened up on one side. Light poured out of it, covering the wall in an eerie white glow. Josh stood there, squinting, trying to figure out why there was no picture.

The sound of footsteps in the hallway broke through his concentration. "Ellen, is that you? Come quick!"

Ellen poked her head through the doorway. She flipped her long brown hair over her shoulder and gave Josh a mischievous look, her brown eyes sparkling. "What's up?"

"The time stone turned on, but there's no picture. I think it's broken."

She hurried into the room and stared at the wall. "You're right. Something's wrong. Go get Will."

Josh slid down the banister and ran into the kitchen. Will was sitting at the table, working his way through a mound of fresh chocolate-chip cookies as he studied for his science test. Their mother glanced at Josh before bending down to take another pan of cookies out of the oven.

Josh leaned over Will's shoulder and whispered in his ear, grabbing a handful of cookies along the way. "Come upstairs, quick. The time stone just turned on."

Will spun around to face Josh, his eyes wide with shock. "What? Now? No way. I'm not going anywhere!" he gasped.

"What did you say, Will?" Their mother was busy sliding another tray of cookies into the oven.

"Nothing," answered Josh, trying to sound like Will. "Come on, Will," he whispered. "There's light, but there's no picture. It's weird. Ellen told me to get you." He grabbed Will by the arm and dragged him toward the stairs.

"Let go of me. I'm coming," hissed Will.

Josh let go. "Good. I just wanted to make sure." He bounded up the stairs two at a time. Will plodded along behind him.

"Hurry up," urged Josh from the landing halfway up. "We don't have all day."

"I'm coming. Give me a minute, will you? I need to psych myself up for this. It's a big deal going on these stupid trips. I was hoping we'd have a longer break."

Josh moved to one side, giving Will room to pass by. "It's been weeks since our last trip," he muttered, more to himself than anyone else, as he pushed his brother the rest of the way up the stairs. "Can't you hurry up?"

Once Will was finally in the bedroom, Josh closed the door behind them. "What if Mom walks in right now? That would be terrible," grumbled Will. He ran his hand across the top of his head, fingering his new brush cut. Josh reached behind Will and locked the door.

"He's right. How would we ever explain this?" said Ellen, motioning to the wall with a flourish.

A long, narrow Viking ship covered the boys' wall. An evil-looking serpent graced its bow, its long neck overshadowing the men unloading cargo onto a pebbly beach. One of the Vikings looked at them with brilliant blue eyes. Josh felt a shiver run up his spine; it seemed like the man could actually see him.

The three of them watched as the picture faded. An enormous pyramid nestled in the desert replaced it. As they stood there, entranced by the sight, the scene moved in closer and closer until they could see a long procession of people winding its way through the dunes to a small opening on the side of the pyramid.

Josh jumped up and down. "Let's go there! That would be perfect! I've always wanted to go to Egypt." He reached out to touch the stone. Will grabbed him by the arm and held his hand back, his grip surprisingly strong.

"What are you doing? Let go of me!" shouted Josh.

"No. We need to see all the pictures before we decide."

"But this one looks good," insisted Josh.

"It might not be the best one. We're going to look at them all."

"Let go of my arm. You're hurting me!"

Will shook his head. "I don't trust you." He squeezed Josh's arm a bit tighter. Josh rolled his eyes in response.

Their discussion ended when the picture vanished and the wall turned completely white. "See? This is how it started. I think the stone's broken," said Josh.

"That's what I thought at first, but when you went to get Will, I studied the picture more closely. If you look really closely you can see a slight variation in the color." Ellen traced a squiggly line along the wall and then pointed to two dark spots. "See those little blobs? I think they're the eyes of an animal."

"What kind of place would be completely white like that?" asked Josh.

"Isn't it obvious?" gloated Will.

"No," replied the other two in unison.

"It's the Arctic."

"Why didn't I think of that?" said Josh.

"Because you're dumb." Will gave Josh and Ellen a smug grin.

Josh tried to pull his arm away. Will responded by squeezing even tighter. "Whatever you do, don't touch the stone right now. I'm not interested in going anywhere that's freezing cold."

"I suppose," agreed Josh. He smiled when a mountain appeared before them. The bottom two-thirds was lush and green, but its top was bare. Nothing appeared to be growing on the desolate windswept rock. Wispy white clouds drifted by, temporarily obscuring the peak. "What about that one?"

"But it looks like a jungle," said Will.

"So?"

"Remember what happened the last time we were at a jungle?"

"You threw up every five minutes," said Josh.

"And we met Luna and Puma and had a fabulous adventure," added Ellen.

"That's one way of looking at it. All I remember is getting sick and being scared. It was horrible. I'm never going to another jungle again."

"I kind of liked it," said Ellen.

"Well, I didn't. There's no way I'm going back. If we wait, something better will come along."

Josh cast his brother a sideways glance. Will was so busy looking at the picture on the wall that he had forgotten about keeping Josh's hand away from the stone. "On the count of three," he whispered to himself. "One … two …" Josh jerked away from Will's grip and flung his body across the bed, barely reaching the stone. As he squeezed his fingers around it, he felt a familiar tingle zip through his body. A whirlwind swooped into their bedroom drowning Will's screams and scooped them up, hurling them back in time.

TWO

THE SOUTH PACIFIC

Josh slowly opened his eyes, wondering what he would find. He was lying on the ground with Will nearby on his left. Before he could gather his thoughts, Will rolled toward him and whacked him on the arm.

Josh rubbed the spot, trying to ease the pain. "What was that for?"

"That's payback for touching the stone. I told you I didn't want to come here, but you didn't listen. You always do whatever you want. You don't care about anyone else."

"Ellen wanted to come; I could tell. It was two against one. Besides, you never want to go anywhere." The quiet buzzing of an insect caught his attention. He sat up and looked around. They had landed in a grove of the strangest looking trees Josh had ever seen. Long, fat roots criss-crossed the ground, the gaps between them filled with flattened leaves. The lower parts of their trunks were bare, but higher up the branches spread out like the spindly legs of a spider. Thick vines joined the ground to the treetops. The sound of running water tinkled from some-where deep inside the forest, and the heavy smell of rotting vegetation filled the warm, damp air.

"Wh …Wh …Where in the world are we?" asked Josh, struggling

to his feet. "This looks like something out of a *Star Wars* movie."

"I don't know, I don't like it, and it's all your fault," moaned Will, sitting up slowly. "Where's Ellen?"

"I'm right here." Ellen lay on her back, propped up on her elbows under one of the trees.

The boys lurched over to her, still dizzy from their journey. Will was in such a hurry to get to Ellen that he forgot to look where he was going. His foot connected with a giant tree root and he sailed through the air, arms flailing and glasses flying, before landing on the ground.

With one hand cradling his nose, he slowly stood up. Blood poured down his lips and chin. Josh and Ellen gave each other a knowing look.

"You need to watch where you're going," said Ellen. She picked up Will's glasses and wiped them on her shirt before handing them back to him.

"No, Josh needs to watch where we time travel." Will was pinching the bridge of his nose, leaning forward to keep blood from dripping on his shirt. He sounded like he had a bad cold. "This is all his fault. I told him I didn't want to come here. This is going to be just like our first jungle trip—I can feel it already—and we all know how badly that one went."

"Come on, Will, stop complaining. We would have come here sooner or later; we've seen this place on your wall before. You need to quit blaming Josh for everything that happens. If you spent less time complaining maybe we could have a good time once in a while."

Will pulled a cotton handkerchief out of his pocket and carefully wiped the blood off his face. Scowling, he looked down at his stained handkerchief, jammed it into his pocket, and stalked out of the clearing with Ellen fluttering by his side.

Josh trailed a safe distance behind, taking care to stay out of Will's way until he cooled off. "Why does he blame me for everything?" he muttered to himself. "And how come he's the only person I know who carries a cloth handkerchief? Hasn't he ever heard of wiping your nose on your sleeve?"

Josh had rejoined his siblings by the time they arrived at the edge of a river. They turned upstream, taking in the lush tree-covered mountain that lay before them. Josh followed the path of the river as it wound its way through the craggy valley, disappearing somewhere on the other side of the mountain, and then turned his gaze upward. Puffs of smoke rose above the barren mountain peak, just like the picture that appeared on their wall. They continued walking in silence. After a few minutes, the valley narrowed and they came to a waterfall. Three pools had formed one beneath the other, slowing the turbulent water to a gentle stream that meandered off into the jungle. Mist rose above each of the pools, coating the leaves and flowers growing along the riverbank with tiny droplets of moisture.

"Wow, it sure is beautiful here," said Ellen. "Where do you think we are?"

"I vote for Central America. This looks exactly like the first jungle we time traveled to—you know, the one I didn't want to go back to," grumbled Will.

"What if we're in Africa?" said Josh, choosing to ignore his brother's sarcastic response. "Maybe we'll see some elephants."

"You have no idea what you're talking about. This doesn't look anything like Africa. It's dry there—they have deserts—it's not green like this at all."

"It is so," protested Josh. "They have a huge waterfall. I've seen pictures of it. It's bigger than Niagara Falls, and it has lots of plants around it, just like this one."

"Is that Victoria Falls you're talking about?" asked Will.

Josh frowned. "Maybe. Why?"

"Because it's one of the biggest waterfalls in the world, and for your information, it doesn't look anything like this," smirked Will.

Ellen stepped forward until she was standing between the two of them. "I'm getting tired of this," she said, looking Will in the eye. "Any chance we can declare a truce?"

"Why are you asking me?"

"Because you're in one of your moods and it's driving me crazy. You know how our time travel works; we've done it four times. Every single time your attitude has been a problem. Do you think you could bury it so we can get on with things?"

"What things?" asked Will.

"The reason we came here, stupid!" interrupted Josh. Ellen shot him a dirty look. "We were sent here to do something, so let's go do it!"

Will stood still, his mouth twitching. "Okay," he agreed, begrudgingly, "but Josh has to promise not to touch the stone unless we all agree. Okay?"

Josh rolled his eyes. "Why did I have to get the most difficult brother in the entire world? And if that wasn't bad enough, we had to be twins." He glanced over at Ellen. She gave him a gentle smile before putting her finger up to her lips. He rolled his eyes again. "Yeah, yeah, I know. Don't worry. I'll be good."

The kids tried to climb up a well-worn path along the riverbank, but it was so wet that progress was difficult. For every two steps forward Josh slid back one, but he managed to stay in the lead. He couldn't help but envy his siblings' sneakers; they provided just enough traction to make the path manageable. Will and Ellen had been wearing shoes when the time stone went off, but Josh wasn't that lucky. He always chose to be barefoot at home so he was barefoot here, too.

They had only been climbing five minutes when Josh's muscles began to ache. His legs and feet were covered in mud. The only time he was able to make better progress was when there were branches and vines growing close to the path. If he grabbed onto them he could pull himself forward and take bigger steps.

After a few more minutes Josh plopped down on the middle of the path, his legs burning. Within seconds Ellen and Will were right beneath him. They stood there, giving their legs a rest as they took in their surroundings.

Finally, Ellen spoke. "We never did figure out where we are. Do you guys have any new ideas?"

"I still think we're in Central America," said Will.

Josh furrowed his brow as he pondered Will's answer. "Why would the time stone send us to the same place twice?" He struggled to his feet and continued up the path. Will and Ellen stayed close behind.

"Just because we're in Central America doesn't mean we're in the exact same place," observed Will. "That's just like saying that every place in our country, Canada, is the same. Being in British Columbia isn't anything like being in Saskatchewan."

"I suppose," agreed Josh.

"I don't know why I think this, but my gut instinct is that we're in the South Pacific. Something about the picture on our wall reminded me of that part of the world," said Ellen. "Maybe it was the shape of the mountain; I don't know. We could be on an island. I've read that there are lots of islands in that part of the world."

Will stopped so suddenly that Ellen almost crashed into him. He looked at her, his face as white as a sheet. "I hope you're wrong."

"Why? What's wrong with the South Pacific? Isn't that where all the good surfing is?" asked Josh.

Will shook his head. "There's something you're forgetting."

"What?"

"Don't you remember who was in the South Pacific?"

Josh pressed his fingers into the sides of his head. "I should know this. Think, think, think." He stood there, motionless, before looking back at his brother. "I don't know. I give up."

Will leaned in closer. "Captain Cook," he whispered.

"Captain Cook?" squealed Josh. "What's he got to do with any-thing?"

"Shh! Be quiet! What if Captain Cook is around here? He might be listening," hissed Will.

Ellen rolled her eyes. "Quit being a drama king. Why are you get-ting so worked up?"

"Don't you remember what happened to him?" asked Will.

She and Josh shook their heads.

"He came to Hawaii by ship and had a big fight with the people living there. He killed one of their kings so they killed him, burned his skin, and kept his bones. They say some people accidentally ate his liver and heart."

"Yuck. That's disgusting," said Ellen, holding her hand over her mouth.

"Why would they keep his bones?" asked Josh. "Shouldn't they have buried them or something?"

"Beats me. It doesn't make any sense to me either, but I think we should be very careful, just in case. You never know what might happen."

"Don't worry, Will. No one would want your bones. They're not that exciting." Josh glanced at Ellen, twirled his finger in a circle at the side of his head, pointed at Will, and mouthed the word "cuckoo."

Will stuck out his tongue at Josh. "Think whatever you want. If we meet anyone, I'm going to be careful, just in case."

After another hour of climbing they reached a meadow at the top of the waterfall. The river seemed to disappear above the falls, so Josh scouted around until he found the source of the water—it poured from an opening in the side of the mountain. The boys collapsed onto the ground and lay on their backs, surveying the spindly trees that grew up the side of the mountain and the thick plants growing around them. Many of the plants had brilliantly colored flowers; the reds and pinks were a startling contrast to the deep green foliage.

Ellen sank to the ground beside them. "What should we do now?"

"We're staying right here," said Will. "I don't see any other paths and you never know what might be lurking in the jungle. For all we know, a panther could be hiding behind those bushes."

"I don't care. I'm not afraid of your imaginary panther. I bet there's a path in there. Come on, Ellen, let's take a look." Josh and Ellen trudged across the meadow to the edge of the rainforest, trying to find an opening.

Will stood up in the middle of the clearing so he could watch them. "Be careful," he shouted. "There could be poisonous snakes in there."

Suddenly, Ellen let out a shriek and jumped back, trembling.

"What's going on?" Will gasped.

"It's a … It's a …" Ellen held her breath and backed away as Josh stuck his head beneath a giant leaf.

"What's going on?" repeated Will.

Ellen didn't reply. A minute later, Josh straightened up and walked over to them.

"What did you see?" asked Will.

"Bones," whispered Josh. "Dried out old bones from some long-dead explorers. They might be from Captain Cook."

All the colored drained from Will's face. "Really?"

"He's just joking. It was a spider," said Ellen, still shaking despite the heat. "You know how much I hate spiders."

"It was the coolest thing I've ever seen. You guys should come see it. It was bright yellow and had red and black markings on its back in a happy face pattern. I've never seen anything like it," said Josh.

Will wiped the sweat off his brow with the corner of his handkerchief. "No thanks. I'll pass."

"What do we do now?" asked Ellen. "Even if we find a path, there's no way I'm going back in there. There could be hundreds of spiders."

"Or maybe thousands," suggested Will. "Let's look for the time stone. If we find it, we can go home."

Josh groaned. "You are such a slow learner. Number one, you know the stone doesn't reappear until it's time for us to go home. We haven't done anything yet so there's no way it's time to go back yet. And number two, we're always sent on these trips for a reason. Why don't we figure out what that reason is and get going? The sooner we start, the sooner we're done."

"That's easy for you to say. You like spiders," said Ellen.

"I'm with Ellen. I think we should try to find the stone so we can go home. Remember how badly our last jungle trip went?" added Will.

"How could we forget? You keep mentioning it every two seconds," said Josh.

"I do not. You're not the one who had to walk along that horrible path through the jungle with a machete at your neck, and you're not the one who almost got trapped in the shaman's lair because your dumb brother kept touching things, and you're not the one …"

"Okay, okay. We get the picture," interrupted Ellen. "We were there too, remember? The last thing we need right now is another fight. Let's make a plan."

"How are we supposed to do that? We never agree on anything. That's what Mom always says," said Josh.

"She's right," replied Will. "If Mom says we can share one bag of potato chips, you always want a different flavor than everybody else. And when we get to watch TV, you always want cartoons, Ellen wants sports, and I want the nature channel."

"We get the picture," repeated Ellen. "If you'd spend less time complaining maybe we could actually do something, like make a plan."

Josh pushed his hair away from his eyes. "That's not going to work."

"Come on, guys. Can't you cooperate, just for a minute?"

"I don't know. It doesn't usually …" Will's voice trailed off as he looked past Josh and Ellen. They turned and spotted a girl about Josh and Will's age creeping through the grass toward them. She had dark brown eyes and skin and a long nose, slightly flat at its tip. A long piece of cloth was tied around her chest, forming a loose dress, and her dark hair hung in waves down to her waist. She carried a tall spear in one hand.

"What do we do now?" whispered Will.

"Stand still. Let her come to us," ordered Ellen.

The three of them watched the girl make her way over to them. When she stood about ten steps away, she dropped her spear, fell face to the ground, and lay motionless.

Josh didn't know what to do. His eyes darted back and forth between the girl and Ellen. He kept looking in the direction of the jungle where he thought she had come from. There was no sign of anyone else. Eventually he caught Ellen's eye and mouthed the words, "What do we do?"

Ellen cleared her throat. "Um, excuse me."

The girl slowly lifted her head and looked up at them.

"It's okay. You can get up."

The girl shook her head and returned her gaze to the ground.

"This isn't good. We need to get out of here," whispered Will.

"Why? She's not doing anything," said Josh.

"That's exactly my point. Look at that spear. What if she turns on us?"

Josh rolled his eyes. "She's not going to hurt us. Watch." He walked over to the girl and gently put his hand on her arm. "It's okay. You can get up. We don't mind."

The girl froze at his touch. She wouldn't look at him.

"Really, it's okay. You can get up now," insisted Josh.

She slowly rose to her feet, picked up her spear, and handed it to Josh.

He shook his head. "No thanks. You keep it." She pushed it closer. "No, really, I don't need a spear. You keep it."

"Take it, Josh. She wants you to have it," said Ellen.

He reluctantly took the spear. It felt solid in his hand. "What are we supposed to do now?" he whispered to Ellen.

"Come with me," said the girl.

Josh gulped. "Did you hear that?"

Ellen nodded. "What's your name?"

"Pilikia."

"*Pee-lee-kee-yah?*" exclaimed Josh. "Who'd want to have a name with 'pee' in it?" Ellen shot him a dirty look. Realizing how rude his question sounded, he smacked his hand against his mouth. "Sorry. I didn't mean it like that. It's just that I've never heard a name like that before."

"Please come to my village," said the girl.

"I'm not going anywhere until someone tells me what's going on," grumbled Will.

Josh pursed his lips together as he glared at his brother. "Hello, earth calling Will. Where have you been? We just met a girl who probably lives around here and she invited us to her village. That's all we know, unless you have some secret knowledge that the rest of us don't have. We've been through stuff like this before on our other trips. What's the big deal?"

"What if it's not safe?" he whined.

"There's only one way to find out. I'm going," said Ellen. She and Josh followed the girl through the tall grass. Will stood in the clearing all by himself, trying to decide what to do.

After a few moments he let out a deep sigh and trudged after them. "Ready or not, here I come."

THREE

BECOMING GODS

❁❂❁❂❁❂❁❂❁❂❁❂❁❂❁

As Josh and Ellen trekked through the rainforest, they peppered Pilikia with questions.

"Does this place have a name?" asked Ellen.

"My people call our island *Havaiki* in honor of our original homeland in the west. After we die our spirits fly back to the ancient homeland of our ancestors."

"Hmm. That word sounds a lot like Hawaii. Maybe that's where we are. Maybe we really are in the South Pacific," said Ellen.

"How did your people get here?" asked Josh.

"My people came here by boat and made new homes on the island."

"How many people are in your family?" asked Ellen.

"Just four: me, my mother, father, and grandmother. We have our own hut in the village," said the girl. "My father is a fisherman, and my mother tends the sweet potato beds. My grandmother is a healer."

"What about you? What kind of chores do you do?"

"I help my mother and grandmother. My grandmother wants to pass her secrets on to me so I can be a healer in our village someday."

Just then, Will caught up to them. "Did you learn anything

important?" he asked his brother and sister.

"I think we're in Hawaii," replied Josh, "but I'm not sure when."

"Have you seen any big ships nearby?" Will asked Pilikia.

"No."

"Ever heard of someone named Captain Cook?"

She shook her head.

"Cook came in the late 1700s. It must be before then. Where's your village?" he asked.

"Halfway up the mountain," said Pilikia, pointing to the mountain with the smoke coming out of the top. The grass huts of her village were barely visible through an opening in the trees. Even though it was clear and sunny where they stood, the top of the mountain was enveloped by a mass of clouds.

"Have you ever climbed up to the top?" asked Josh.

Pilikia stopped in her tracks and stared at him, horrified. "I'd never go up there. *Pele* lives there. I wouldn't want to make her angry. Only the priests can go to the top."

"Who's *Pay-lay*?"

"Um, excuse me," interrupted Will, looking pale again. "Did I hear that right? Did you say that Pele lives on top of that mountain?"

Pilikia slowly nodded.

"Are we talking about Pele, the goddess of the volcano?"

Pilikia nodded again.

Will gulped. "I want to go home."

"You mean that's a volcano?" asked Josh, jumping up and down as he pointed at the mountaintop. "Wow! This is great!" He pranced around the clearing chanting, "We're at a volcano! We're at a volcano!"

Will clasped his arms tightly against his chest. "Wh …Wh …When was the last time that volcano erupted?"

"Not since long before my great-great-grandparents' time," Pilikia replied.

"Is that good or bad?" asked Ellen.

Pilikia shrugged her shoulders.

"It's bad," said Will. "The longer a volcano is quiet, the worse its explosion can be."

"And how do you know that, Mr. Volcano Expert?" asked Josh.

"For your information, I'm not a volcanologist, but I do happen to know a lot about volcanoes. One of the worst ones on record was at Krakatoa, just off the coast of Java, an island in Indonesia. It was so big that people in Australia and India could hear its explosion, and it created tsunami waves that killed almost forty thousand people. The dust from it circled around the earth for years, making the temperature drop and changing the way sunsets appeared.

"The volcano most people know about is Mount Vesuvius. When it erupted in 79 AD, the whole town of Pompeii was buried in volcanic ash. It wasn't unearthed until excavations began in the sixteenth century. The archeologists were amazed at what they found—the ash covered everything when it buried the town, preserving a perfect record of life back then."

"How do you know all that? You could make all that stuff up and we'd never know it."

"For your information—"

"—Let me guess," Josh interrupted. "You read it in a book."

Will gave him a triumphant smile. "How did you know I'd say that?"

"You've only said it nine hundred times before."

"You don't need to worry. My people take offerings to Pele every day. She's happy; nothing bad is going to happen," said Pilikia.

"We don't need to worry? You live on the side of the mountain underneath a volcano and we don't need to worry? You know what I think?" Will took a deep breath and held it in for a few seconds. "I think you're all crazy." He pushed his way past Ellen, Josh, and Pilikia and stalked up the path.

Two minutes later Will was back, panting and crying. He ran over to Ellen, almost knocking her to the ground. She wrapped her arms around him to steady him. "What's wrong?" she asked.

"This is going to be a terrible trip; I just know it. We're going to die out here. We're never going back."

"What on earth are you talking about?"

"There's lava up ahead. It must have oozed out of the mountain and made a little clearing." Will sunk to the ground in a crumpled heap. "We need to get out of here before that volcano kills us."

Josh stepped over his brother and ran up the path. "Where are you going?" shouted Ellen.

"To see the lava. Come on!"

Josh raced up the path with Ellen and Pilikia close behind. It took only a minute to reach the clearing. Josh looked around expectantly. All he could see was a wide swath of the strangest jet-black rock he'd ever seen. Swirls and dips ran through it, twirling every which way possible as it made a path through the clearing.

Will crept up behind them. "See what I mean? That's lava. Be careful."

Josh scratched the side of his head as he scanned the clearing. "I don't see any lava."

"That black rock you're standing on is lava."

Josh looked down at the rock beneath his feet. "This is lava? This is what you got all excited about?"

"I thought lava was supposed to be orange and hot. Are you sure you know what you're talking about?" asked Ellen.

Will glared at her. "Sometimes lava turns smooth and black like this when it hardens. It can also be really jagged. You won't be able to walk on that type barefoot, Josh."

"And how do you know ... oh, never mind. How could I forget? You probably read it in a book," muttered Josh.

Will leaned in closer to his brother and sister so Pilikia couldn't hear him. "That girl said the volcano was okay, but this lava proves it's erupted before. I don't think we should go anywhere near her village. If it erupts again, we're goners."

Josh looked around at the hardened rock. Clumps of ferns and trees were growing in some of its cracks. "This lava looks pretty old to me. I think it's been here for a long time. You're getting all worked about nothing."

"I agree. Besides, God will protect us. He always has before," added Ellen.

"Fine. If we have any volcano problems, I'm blaming them on you. And you had better promise not to be mad when I say 'I told you so.'"

"Whatever," muttered Josh. He was too busy enjoying their adventure to worry about the volcano. "Let's go."

It took the kids a couple of hours to work their way up and around the mountain to the outskirts of Pilikia's village. Josh and Pilikia led the way, chattering as if they had known each other for years. Ellen and Will followed a few steps behind. Occasionally, Josh could hear Ellen scolding Will or encouraging him. *I'm glad I don't have to listen to him for a while,* thought Josh.

By the time they arrived at the building that guarded the entrance to the village, they were exhausted. Will sank to the ground next to the stick fence that surrounded it, his head resting on his knees. Josh was worn out too; his legs felt like they were on fire, but he was so excited that he couldn't sit still. He and Ellen paced along the fence, peering between the narrow openings. Josh was able to catch a glimpse of the rectangular platform of rocks that formed the base of the building. Its thatched roof provided protection from the sun and rain, and its sides were open so the breeze could flow through. There appeared to be people and objects inside, but Josh couldn't tell who or what they were. If there was a way into the building, he couldn't see it. The fence appeared to completely surround it.

He stepped back and spotted a series of houses behind the building. They looked sturdy, with similar rock bases and thatched roofs, except they had dried straw on their sides for protection and privacy.

At first glance, it seemed like the houses had been plunked down wherever the people felt like building them, but as Josh scanned the village he realized there was a certain order to it all. Some of the houses were grouped around groves of trees and others around small ponds. Still others were arranged in rough circles around piles of leaves and bigger huts.

The villagers moved about as they worked. Josh spotted a group of women weaving long leaves into baskets and men carving bowls out of wood. He watched four men step out of a hut where something that looked like a canoe was being built. They lifted the front end of the canoe and pulled it forward before disappearing back into the hut.

Josh turned toward Pilikia to ask her about the canoe when three men walked out of the building. "It's the priest," whispered Pilikia.

The priest was simply clothed in a long white robe, a perfect match to his white hair. He had the look of man who had spent hours in the sun; deep wrinkles surrounded his eyes and mouth and were etched across his forehead. His head was bare except for the fringe of hair that bordered the bottom of his scalp.

The two men with him were a striking contrast; they were young with full heads of hair and muscular bodies. One of them grabbed the priest's arm when he stopped at the top of the stairs, hesitating before he took the first step down. The three of them were halfway down the steps when they spotted Josh and his siblings on the other side of the fence. The priest let out a shriek and stumbled, landing on the ground at the bottom of the steps. His assistants ran over to him and lay flat on their faces on either side of him. Pilikia dropped to the ground next to Josh, Will, and Ellen.

Josh glanced at his brother and sister; both of them looked confused. "Ellen, do something," he whispered.

Ellen stepped up to the fence and stood on her tiptoes, allowing her to barely see over it. "You can get up," she called out, motioning with her hands for the men to rise. The priest struggled to his feet and stepped backward, moaning loudly as he moved away from the fence toward the building.

One of the villagers who had heard the priest's cry came running through the village, shouting as he went. Within minutes a sea of dark-skinned people were huddled behind them, silently watching Josh, Will, and Ellen's every move. The priest's assistants stood up, opened a hidden gate in the fence, and guided Josh and his siblings into the temple, moving carefully so they didn't touch them in the process. Once the gate was closed, the villagers rushed over to the fence so they could see what was happening.

As Josh made his way toward the stairs, he passed a row of sticks between the fence and the temple. They had been planted in the ground at regular intervals. A shiver ran down his spine when he realized that each post had a human skull perched on top of it.

Will grabbed Josh's arm. "Did you see those skulls?"

Josh nodded. "They're giving me the creeps. I hope Ellen didn't see them. What if they want our skulls?" he asked, his teeth chattering.

"I knew we shouldn't have come here," moaned Will.

Josh gasped as they passed through the doorway. A series of five life-size wooden statues were arranged in a semicircle around a small wooden table at the far end of the room. Each statue had a ghastly face with huge swollen lips and vacant eyes. The middle statue had a red cloth wrapped around its neck like a bandanna.

The priest led them over to the statues. Goose bumps broke out over Josh's skin, surprising considering the heat of the day. He could feel his stomach churning. Everything about this temple felt wrong, but he didn't know what to do about it.

The priest began chanting. His assistants joined in and helped him drape red cloths around Josh, Will, and Ellen's shoulders. Then the priest walked over to the statue with the bandanna and kissed its wooden lips. He turned to the kids and motioned for them to do the same.

"I'm not kissing that carving. That's disgusting," muttered Josh.

"We'd better cooperate; we don't want to offend them," whispered Ellen.

"But what if that means we're worshiping a false god?"

"I don't think that's what we're doing. For all we know, those carvings might mean nothing." Ellen walked over to the wooden statue, carefully skirting the low wooden table in front of it, and gave its thick lips a delicate kiss.

The priest looked at Josh and Will, waiting for them to take their turns. Josh looked at Ellen, grimaced, and walked over to the idol. He waited until he thought no one was looking and gave the idol a tiny peck of a kiss. It was over so quickly the priest almost missed it. The priest gave him an approving smile and turned to Will, expectantly.

"It's no big deal. Hurry up and get it over with," urged Ellen.

Will began to shake uncontrollably. "I'm not kissing that hunk of wood."

"What's the big deal?" asked Josh. "It's just a stupid kiss. It won't hurt you."

"No way. I'm not kissing that thing."

"Come on, Will. It's no big deal. Josh and I both kissed it and nothing happened to us," said Ellen.

Will crossed his arms and pulled them tightly against his chest. "Nothing has happened to you *yet*. I don't kiss idols," he said, getting louder, "and you shouldn't have either, so quit bugging me about it."

Ellen looked over to the priest. "Sorry. He won't do it."

The priest walked to the back of the room and returned a minute later with a dead pig cradled in his arms. Its mottled skin was pulled tight by the bloated muscles underneath and the smell coming from it was atrocious, definitely way worse than the smell from Josh's lunch kit after he'd left it under his bed all summer with a half-eaten salami, peanut butter, and pickle sandwich inside.

The priest lovingly placed the pig on the table in front of the idols.

His assistants arranged sugarcane, coconuts, sweet potatoes, and some strange-looking fruit around the animal.

Josh's nose began to twitch; the stench was so bad he didn't want to breathe. He made a nasty face at his brother. "Way to go, Will. If you had kissed the statue like me and Ellen, they wouldn't have brought this disgusting pig in here."

He glanced over at Ellen. She had turned a grayish-green and was standing with her eyes closed and her hand over her mouth, trying not to gag. Josh wasn't surprised by her reaction. As a vegetarian, she was especially sensitive about dead animals.

Once the pig and the fruit and vegetables were perfectly arranged, the priest stepped back and spoke in a garbled language Josh couldn't understand. The final words were barely out of his mouth when his assistants lifted the table and carried it out of the temple. The priest motioned for Josh, Will, and Ellen to follow them. He ended the procession two steps behind them.

Excited murmuring filtered through the crowd when the kids came into view. They followed the priest's assistants over to the stick fence and watched as they lifted the table and hurled the pig over it. It landed on the ground with a splat.

Josh leaned over to Ellen. "That was weird."

"I'm relieved we don't have to look at it anymore. It made me feel sick."

The priest led the kids to the side of the temple and began chanting again. They stood beside him overlooking the people. As the chanting droned on, several villagers cautiously walked through the gate and handed each of the kids a squirming piglet. Josh smiled as he accepted his; he liked animals. He clutched it tightly in his arms, rocking back and forth. Before long the little animal was asleep, its snout nestled underneath Josh's elbow.

Josh turned to watch Will, who was trying to refuse his piglet. The villager holding it out in front of him wouldn't relent. He glanced over to Ellen, looking for reassurance. She glared at Will until he reluctantly held out his arms and accepted his gift. Ellen smiled as she took hers; she liked animals as long as she didn't have to eat them.

A second procession of villagers came forward and set down a fresh roasted hog as well as some pudding, fruit, coconuts, and other vegetables. The kids sat cross-legged on the landing with the piglets in their laps. Josh watched the priest cut up the hog. One of the assistants began peeling the vegetables and the other worked with the coconuts. The man cracked the first one open, grabbed a large piece of the white nut meat, popped it in his mouth, chewed it, and spit it into a cloth. Then he walked over to Josh and began rubbing the chewed-up coconut all over Josh's face, hands, and arms.

Josh dropped his piglet and scurried back, trying to get away. The piglet woke up and squealed as it ran off into the village. The man firmly grabbed Josh's arm and continued rubbing coconut on his face.

Josh tried to push his hand out of the way. "What do you think you're doing? Leave me alone."

The man ignored him and continued wiping the goopy mixture all over Josh's exposed skin. Ellen and Will watched from the side of the temple, horrified. When the man was finished with Josh, he popped another piece of coconut into his mouth, chewed it up, spit it into the cloth, and walked over to Will.

"Oh, no, you don't," said Will, backing away. "You're not putting any of that gunk on me."

The man tried to grab Will by the arm, but Will wouldn't cooperate. He kept pushing the man's hand away. Eventually, the other assistant came over and pinned Will to the ground. He thrashed and hollered and cried as they quickly spread the coconut all over his body. When they were finished, Will crawled away and curled up like a baby, sobbing.

The two assistants looked at Ellen. "If I were you, I'd cooperate," said Josh. "Fighting back sure didn't help Will."

Ellen stood there, motionless, her arms and legs extended as the assistants repeated the process with her. When they were done, they stepped back to admire their handiwork. Josh stood beside her, not sure what he should do. Will stayed curled upon the ground, crying.

The priest approached them, sparing Josh from making a decision. He motioned for Will to get up and join the others. Will reluctantly got to his feet and plodded over to Josh and Ellen. The priest handed each of them a strip of meat. Josh turned his over and inspected it. Little bits of singed hair were stuck to the skin.

"What are we supposed to do with this?" mumbled Will.

"I think we're supposed to eat it. You might want to pick the skin off first," suggested Josh.

Will examined his piece more closely. "I don't want to eat this. What if it's not cooked all the way? You can get worms from eating raw meat."

Josh flicked his piece with his finger. "It looks cooked to me."

"But you eat everything."

Josh took a bite. "It's pretty good. Try it."

"No thanks." Will put his piece down on the ground. The priest motioned for him to pick it up. Will shook his head. "No thanks. I'm not hungry."

The priest picked the meat up from the ground, popped it into his mouth, chewed it for a minute, and then grabbed Will's hand and pried open his fingers. He took the chewed-up meat from his mouth, put it in Will's palm, and forced Will's fingers over it. All the color drained from Will's face. "No, really, I can't eat this," he said, shaking his head.

The priest pried open Will's fingers again, scooped up the chewed-up meat, and lifted it up to Will's mouth. Will clamped his lips shut and covered his mouth with his empty hand as he violently shook his head back and forth.

The priest's hand hovered in the air as he waited for Will to cooperate. Will stood as still as a statue. After a few minutes the priest popped the meat back into his mouth and swallowed.

Now that the initial preparations were complete, the priest led Josh, Will, and Ellen back into the temple. He gave each of them a beautiful cloak, feathered headdress, and a fan. The cloaks were so long that they dragged on the floor and the headdresses were sized for large men, not twelve- and fourteen-year-old kids, but Josh liked his new outfit anyway. He strutted around, trying to look kinglike, but didn't quite succeed. His headdress kept drooping to one side, covering his right eye. Ellen seemed to be comfortable in her new clothing, but Will looked like he'd rather be wearing anything else.

"Come on, Will, be a good sport. They gave us this fancy stuff because they think we're important. We may as well go along with it. I guarantee that nobody at home will think we're royalty or gods or whatever these people think we are. These clothes remind me of the ones we wore when we were in England. You managed just fine there. You can do this," said Josh.

"No, I can't," grumbled Will, "and I didn't manage 'just fine' when we were in England, either. My stupid horse practically killed me and that armor was so uncomfortable. I don't want to be here any more than I wanted to be there. Maybe if I close my eyes and concentrate I'll be able to pretend this isn't happening."

"I wonder if they do think we're gods. That scares me," said Ellen. "Why else would they put these red scarves around our necks? They're treating us the same way they treated those statues."

"All I know is that we need to get out of here and the sooner, the better. Everything feels wrong. I want to go home," said Will.

"Come on, guys, can't you go along with this for a little while?" asked Josh. "It's not that bad."

Will flipped his cloak over his shoulder. "You'd think it was horrible if someone chewed up your food for you."

Josh rolled his eyes. "Whatever. I'll go find out what's happening next." As Josh took a step toward the back of the temple where the priest was talking quietly to his assistants, his foot caught the hem of his cloak and he tripped and fell, landing face down on the hard stone floor. Blood spurted out of a gash on his chin and began pooling on the floor. He let out a loud wail when he spotted the red puddle beneath him. Ellen ran over and helped him to his feet.

A second later the priest and his assistants were beside him. The priest grabbed Josh by the shoulders and lifted him off the ground, holding him midair until they were face-to-face. Josh struggled to get away, but the priest wouldn't let go. "You're hurting me! Leave me alone!" he shouted.

The priest released his grip. Josh stumbled as his feet hit the floor, but he quickly regained his balance. He cupped his chin with one hand and used the other to move his headdress back into place—it was drooping over his eye again—and pushed his cloak back so it wouldn't get dirty from his blood.

"You're not a god," roared the priest, wagging his finger at Josh. "Gods do not feel pain. They do not trip over their cloaks and fall and bleed. You tricked us!"

"I never said I was a god. That was your idea, not mine."

"He's right," added Ellen. "We never said we were gods. Pilikia asked us to come to your village and we agreed. We didn't know what to do when you bowed down to us."

"So, none of you are gods?" cried the priest.

The three of them shook their heads sheepishly.

"Then there is only one solution: The penalty for your deception is death!"

— FOUR —

BIG TROUBLE

The priest's assistants stripped the kids of their cloaks, headdresses, and fans, and herded them out of the temple, shoving them down the steps to the landing where they had stood only minutes before. When the villagers spotted the blood on Josh's chin a hush fell over the crowd. A tall man standing at the back lifted his spear into the air and began yelling. Josh couldn't understand what he was saying, but he could see the crowd transform before his eyes from a gathering of adoring people into an angry mob.

Will began to sway back and forth. Ellen grabbed his arm and tried to steady him. It didn't help. She wrapped her arms around his chest a second before he fainted and eased him to the ground. With this new display of weakness, more shouts erupted from the crowd. The people moved in closer, pressing up against the fence.

"Josh, what should we do?" she cried.

"I don't know. Why does Will always have to faint when things get bad?"

The crowd strained forward. The stick fence began to sway from the pressure of their bodies. Children in the front row shouted insults at Josh and Ellen.

"You're not gods. You're just a bunch of weaklings," cried one.

"Get lost. We don't want you here," yelled another.

Ellen moved closer to Josh. "We need to pray."

"Dear God, please help us," whispered Josh. "We don't know why these people are so mad at us, and we don't know what to do. Please make Will wake up, and don't let anyone hurt us."

Will stirred. His eyes flickered open. He began shaking when he saw the mob pressing toward them.

Just then Josh spotted Pilikia. She was standing near the fence with a man and a woman. *They must be her parents,* he thought. He watched as she spoke to them, waving her hand in their direction. Her father bent down so he could hear what she was saying. Soon her mother was nodding. Pilikia grabbed her father by the hand and pulled him toward the hidden gate in the fence.

Pilikia's father had to push his way through the crowd. When he reached the bottom of the steps he waited for the priest to acknowledge him. Eventually, the priest came down and joined him. The two of them stood together on one of the lower steps, talking. Even though Josh was standing close by, he couldn't hear a thing. The crowd was too noisy. Before long, the priest appeared to be agreeing with Pilikia's father. The two men nodded at each other, and then Pilikia's father returned to his family.

The priest motioned for Josh and Ellen to follow him up the steps. They grabbed Will by the arms and dragged him along until they were back inside the temple.

"Assistants, stay with them until I return," ordered the priest. He spun around and returned to the landing to address his people.

Josh moved toward the doorway. The assistants stayed where they were. Growing bolder, he poked his head around the corner. He could see the priest's back and hear some of what he was saying.

"They never claimed they were gods.... No, we assumed they were because of their strange appearance ... I don't know where they came from.... They could have lost their way as they traveled across the ocean; that has happened to others before.... I haven't heard of any broken canoes along the shoreline, but we haven't had a messenger in some time...."

As the priest continued, the crowd began to calm down. The people along the edges drifted away.

"What are we going to do with them?" shouted a young man near the front.

"Sacrifice them," cackled a wrinkled old woman. "They're no good for anything else."

"I don't want to be a sacrifice," cried Will, who had crept forward. Josh turned around just in time to see his brother's eyes roll back in his head. He slumped to the floor.

The sound of more shouting drew Josh's attention back to the crowd. The priest was looking at Pilikia's father. Pilikia grabbed her father's hand and gazed up at him, her eyes pleading on behalf of her new friends. Eventually, her father spoke. "We should banish them from the village. That is punishment enough."

"But father—" protested Pilikia.

He placed his hand on top of her head. "Enough. It is done."

Six warriors stalked up the steps, their muscles rippling as they moved. One of them grabbed Will and slung him over his shoulder. The others shoved Josh and Ellen toward the door. Before they could blink, the kids were dragged down the stairs. The warriors pushed them off the last step, causing them to trip.

They forced the kids into a line with three warriors in front and three at the back, making sure no one could escape. By now Will was awake and stumbling along with the group. They passed groves of banana and coconut trees, feathery sugarcane plants, and plots of leafy crops surrounded by low stone fences. More stone fences enclosed pens of pigs and chickens. The farther they traveled, the more rugged the terrain became. The sun began to set, making the surrounding rainforest seem darker and spookier than before.

Will turned around and glared at his brother. "This is all your fault. You should have listened to me when I told you not to touch the stone."

As Josh struggled to maneuver through the thick layer of ferns covering the ground, he found himself reluctantly agreeing with his brother. He had to constantly duck under huge fronds taller than he was just to stay on the path. Every so often Ellen stopped and breathlessly waited for Josh to push the leaves back so she could pass by. She was afraid she might find more spiders.

The warriors knew which way to turn every time there was a fork in the path, but Josh quickly lost track of their directions. He'd been trying to memorize their route in case they wanted to return to the village. A lump formed in the pit of his stomach when he realized he couldn't remember how to travel back. "There's no way we'll ever get out of here," he grumbled under his breath. "God, where are you? We asked you to help us, not put us in worse trouble."

The words *I am with you* floated through his head. It was as if a soft voice whispered them in his ear. They were followed by a verse from Psalm 23, part of a Bible passage his church had been memorizing. *Even though I walk through the valley of the shadow of death, I will fear no evil, for you are with me; your rod and your staff, they comfort me.*

Rain began sprinkling down, but the tall trees that towered above them blocked most of the drops. Josh looked up. A gigantic raindrop landed right in his eye. *Is this your idea of a joke, God? Because if it is, I don't think it's funny. I don't want to be here. Give me the time stone so we can go home.*

Josh slowed down and looked around, half expecting the time stone to drop out of the sky and land at his feet. Nothing happened. He noticed the forest was growing quieter. The warrior behind him gave him a push, sending him on his way.

After about an hour of brisk hiking down the mountain the three warriors leading the procession came to an abrupt halt. Their leader turned to Ellen. "This is where we leave you. There's a stream a short ways ahead. Do not return to our village."

"B … B … But what are we supposed to do out here?" stammered Will.

The warrior shrugged. "That's up to you. You're on your own now."

The guards spun around. Within seconds all six of them disappeared down the path and the ferns fell into their original positions, completely obscuring the path.

Josh, Will, and Ellen were completely alone.

As the sun dipped below the horizon, the rainforest grew even darker. "This is horrible," whined Will. "You know I don't like the dark. We need to get out of here."

"But where should we go?" asked Josh.

"I don't know. Anywhere is better than this. This reminds me of the graveyard we slept in in Prague, except it's a hundred times worse."

"This is nothing like that graveyard and you know it. That graveyard was fancy with all those tombstones and that tall fence around it. It's nothing like being stranded in a rainforest at night, stupid," muttered Josh.

"Hey, I heard that. You're not supposed to call me names, especially not that one. I'm not stupid and you know it. I'm very smart."

"Guys," said Ellen, exasperated, "quit fighting. It doesn't help. We need to start praying."

"You're right—" began Will.

"As usual," interrupted Ellen.

He grimaced. "Who's going first?"

"I'm not praying," said Josh. "I tried that earlier, and it didn't do us any good. I don't think God can hear us out here. He's probably too busy with everyone else to listen to us."

Ellen put her hands on her hips and glared at her brother. "Joshua Donald MacKenzie, I can't believe you just said that. God can do whatever he wants. That's why he's God and we're not. In the Bible it says he will always be with us, right until the end of the world. I'm positive that means he's with us right now. Besides, he was with us on all our other adventures."

"I suppose," agreed Josh begrudgingly, "but I'm still not convinced he's here with us right now. What if he decided not to help us anymore? Maybe there's no point in praying. It probably won't do any good, anyhow."

"That's the most horrible thing I've ever heard you say. God doesn't just forget about people and you know it. You need to force those bad thoughts out of your mind and think about good things, like how much God's been with us in the past."

Josh frowned. "Whatever."

The cry of a large bird filled the clearing, followed by a snarl and the violent flapping of wings. Josh moved closer to his brother and sister. The bird cried out again, quieter this time.

"That bird sounds wounded. Maybe we should try to help it," said Ellen.

Will started shaking. He curled his body into a tight ball. "I'm not going anywhere. Whatever attacked that animal might want to hurt us, too."

Josh looked up at his sister, his eyes filled with tears. "If God is with us then why did he abandon us out here?"

— FIVE —

RUSHING WATER

Josh was relieved when morning finally arrived. Once he got used to the noises of the animals moving along the forest floor he had been able to sleep for an hour or two, which was more than Ellen got. She awoke with every tiny sound.

Josh glanced over at his sister. She was sitting on the ground with her head in her hands, groaning. *I bet she has a headache. I should probably be nice to her today.*

He stood and stretched, enjoying the melodies of the birds twittering above him. Heat flooded his cheeks as he remembered what he had said about praying the night before. "I hope Ellen's not mad about that anymore. I was just saying what I thought," he muttered to himself. "You can't blame a guy for that."

Josh was making his way through the tall ferns, trying to find a place to go to the bathroom, when Pilikia appeared from out of nowhere. He was so surprised that he jumped back, smashing his heel on the scaly bark of the tree behind him. "What are you doing here?" he moaned through clenched teeth, hopping up and down as he clutched his foot in his hands.

Pilikia beamed at him. "I'm here to be with you, of course."

"How did you get here?"

"The same way you did, silly."

"The last time I checked, the path had vanished. It's hidden somewhere underneath all those ferns. You should cut them down."

"The path is easy to find if you know where to look for it."

Both of them were quiet for a moment before Josh spoke. "By the way, thanks for coming to our rescue yesterday. That was really great of you to help us out like that."

Pilikia stared at the ground. "I felt bad about everything that happened. It wasn't supposed to work out like that."

"You're a real pal," said Josh, lightly punching her on the arm. "I'm glad to have you as a friend."

Pilikia smiled with relief. "Me, too."

"So, we're friends, right?"

"Sure. That's fine with me. Want me to show you around? I could take you to all my favorite places."

"Okay, but first let's shake on our friendship." Josh put out his fist. He arranged her hand on top of his, followed by his hand, and then her other one on top.

Pilikia looked confused. "Why are we doing this?"

"It's our secret handshake," replied Josh. "On the count of three we throw our arms into the air and shout 'Friends.' Ready?"

Pilikia nodded.

"Good. One … two … th …"

Just then Ellen and Will appeared, interrupting their little ritual. Josh and Pilikia dropped their hands to their sides.

"Pilikia, when did you get here? I thought nobody was allowed to be here with us," said Ellen.

"I told my parents I was going to look for one of our chickens that flew away yesterday. If anyone asks, I just happened to find you. Don't worry, everything will be fine." Pilikia turned and began walking away from the group.

"We were just about to do some exploring. See you guys later," said

Josh, following her.

"Whoa, just a minute. You weren't thinking of going anywhere without us, were you?" asked Will.

"We always stick together," added Ellen.

Josh flipped his hair away from his eyes. "You guys can live without me for a little while. Don't worry. I'll be back."

"But Josh, we always stick together," insisted Ellen.

"She's right. We're coming, too," said Will.

Josh and Pilikia looked at each other. "I guess they can come if they promise not to get in the way," she grumbled. She leaned over to Josh so she could whisper in his ear. "I think it would be more fun if it was just the two of us."

"I agree," he whispered back, "but they're too scared to stay by themselves. Maybe we can go without them tomorrow."

"Why don't we run away? If we run fast enough, we'll easily lose them."

Josh's mouth twitched as he pondered Pilikia's idea. "I don't know. That would probably make them mad."

"Fine," said Pilikia, no longer caring if Will and Ellen heard her. "Go ahead and be a baby; it's your choice."

"I'm not a baby. I'm way tougher than most people, especially Will," protested Josh.

"We'll see about that," said Pilikia. She turned to Will and Ellen. "Come on, everyone. Let's go."

Pilikia led them down the maze of paths that meandered along the rainforest floor. When Josh looked ahead, all he could see were hundreds of green plants. Huge tree ferns with feathery leaves grew alongside low-growing plants like the *ohelo* with its sweet, red berries and the *peperomia* with leaves that tasted like peppermint. Bigger plants like the *sisal* stood tall with tough, spiky leaves. The tall, pale-barked *ohia* trees like the one Josh smashed his heel against towered over them all.

The more Josh listened to Pilikia, the more he realized how much he had not noticed. She showed him a carefully hidden path with signs of recent travel, like broken fern fronds, well-trodden leaves that weren't visible until the forest undergrowth was moved out of the way, and slight scuff marks on some of the tree trunks.

Pilikia moved so fast that the three of them had to hurry to keep up. They hadn't adapted to the thick, moist air that she was used to, which made their journey even harder. Pilikia moved quickly, not wasting a single step. About fifteen minutes into their hike, the sound of rushing water filtered through the forest.

"The guards who took us out here said there was a stream up ahead. Is that what I hear?" asked Josh.

Pilikia nodded, not stopping for even a second. "It's either the stream or the ocean."

"Oh. I was getting thirsty. Come to think of it, I'm kind of hungry, too."

"Surprise, surprise," grumbled Will. "So, what else is new?"

A few steps later they reached the edge of the rainforest. The forest floor gave way to jagged black rock. Instead of a stream, the ocean spread out ahead of them as far as the eye could see. Josh walked up to the edge of the rocks, the stiff wind blowing his blond hair in every direction, and peered down a sheer cliff. The sunlight was blinding and his hair kept getting in his eyes, making it hard to see. He shielded his face with his hand. As the surf crashed into the shore below, large bubbles flew into the air before settling back down onto the waves, eventually washing up along the rocky shoreline.

"Josh, get back here. You're way to close to the edge," shouted Ellen. He reluctantly took a few steps back.

Will didn't go near the cliff, preferring to hang back in the safety of the rainforest. "They should have a guardrail out here, or at the very least, some danger signs," he said.

"You know, this isn't like Disney World or some other tourist attraction. They don't have rules like we have at home," said Ellen.

"Thanks for pointing that out. If you hadn't said anything, I would have thought we were in a giant amusement park, getting ready to go on a roller coaster or some other equally stupid ride."

Ellen scowled at him. "Fine. Have a bad attitude. See if I care."

Josh walked back to his brother and sister. "What's up, guys? You both sound pretty grumpy."

"Oh, nothing much," replied Ellen. "Just our normal fighting. Will's in a bad mood this morning—imagine that. You might want to avoid him whenever possible."

"Whoa. It must be bad. Usually you're the peacemaker, forcing me and Will to get along."

Ellen took a deep breath and blinked rapidly, trying to hold back her tears. "I hope we all feel better tomorrow."

"If we survive until then," added Will.

"I can understand why Will would be grouchy—he's always grouchy on our trips," said Josh. He cocked his head to one side and stared at his sister, trying to figure out what was upsetting her. "Usually you're the happy one who's always cheering everybody up. Are you feeling okay?"

"I'm just tired and hungry, that's all. And it didn't help that you wanted to go off with Pilikia on your own. Maybe if we rest for a while I'll feel better."

Josh gave her an encouraging smile. "I'll rustle up some food." He turned to Pilikia. "Any idea where we can get something to eat and drink? Where's that stream you were telling us about?"

"It's just over the edge," she said, motioning toward the cliff with her hand.

"I didn't see any water, except for the ocean, of course." Josh walked back to the cliff and peered over the edge. About two stories down, he discovered the "stream" Pilikia and the guards had mentioned. A torrent of water poured out of an opening in the side of the cliff. He turned to Pilikia. "The water's a long way down. How are we supposed to get it?"

Pilikia didn't answer. She strode back to the edge of the forest and dug around in the bushes, pushing ferns out of the way until she found what she was looking for—a pail made from a hollowed out tree trunk attached to a long rope of braided vine.

With the end of the rope securely in her hand, she walked to the edge of the cliff, lay down on her stomach with her arms and head dangling over the side, and lowered the pail down the side of the cliff to the waterspout. Once it was full she carefully hoisted it back up and placed it on the ground beside her. Josh and Ellen ran over and dipped their hands in the pail, slurping up the fresh, cool water. Pilikia refilled it and brought it over to Will. Once he had his fill, Josh drank the rest of the bucket.

"That was the best water I've ever tasted." Josh wiped the trickle from his chin with the back of his hand.

"Me, too," agreed Ellen.

Will stood there, staring down at his feet, not saying a word.

"I see someone's still grumpy," said Josh. "Come on, Will, you can admit it. It was good and you know it."

Will tried to scowl, but it didn't work. He reluctantly gave Josh and Ellen a tiny smile.

Ellen sighed, relieved. "Thanks for getting us that water, Pilikia. I think it made everyone feel better."

"I agree," shouted Josh. "I feel great! Pilikia, lead the way. Let's go find some food."

Pilikia led them along the edge of the cliff to the end of a dried-out streambed. It passed through the jungle like a highway on its way to the ocean. She turned and walked up the streambed. Josh followed her for about ten steps, then stopped. The move from the sunny, salt-laden air at the cliff to the dark, heavy air of the rainforest was a shock to his senses. The warm sunlight he had enjoyed only minutes before was blocked by the tree branches that hung over the streambed, making him feel like he was standing in the middle of a damp, shady tunnel. Birds chirped their songs. As he looked around, he caught an occasional glimpse of them fluttering among the treetops.

"We're in another world," he said to himself.

As they trekked along the streambed, Josh's spirits lifted. The rainforest didn't seem quite so muggy when he wasn't so hemmed in by the ferns. "You know, this rainforest isn't half bad when you don't have to wade through all those plants."

"I agree." Will said. "When did you discover this streambed?"

"My family has known about it for generations. This land belongs to my village," said Pilikia, motioning to the forest on either side of her. "It starts on the mountain above the village and extends all the way down to the ocean."

"Wow. That's a pretty big piece," said Josh.

"I know. We have one of the larger portions. It has everything from forests to flatland for crops to fish in the ocean."

Just then Josh spotted a grove of banana trees growing along the side of the streambed. "Food," he shouted, running toward the trees. He grabbed a green banana from one of the lower bunches, pulled hard until it ripped off the tree, tore off the peel, and shoved it into his mouth. "Bananas!" he whooped. "I love bananas!"

Will and Ellen watched as Josh grabbed three more bananas and did a zany dance in the middle of the streambed. He was so busy gobbling down the bananas that he didn't notice Pilikia standing with her back toward him.

Josh's dance came to a halt as the last piece of banana slid down his throat. "Whew! That was good. I was so hungry." He flashed Will and Ellen a satisfied smile. "You guys want some?"

"They didn't look ripe," said Will.

"Who cares? At least they're food." Josh ran back to the grove, pulled off a bunch as long as his legs, and dragged them over to the others. "Take one," he said, holding out a small green banana to Will.

Will gingerly pulled down the peel and took a cautious bite. "Hmm. It's better than I thought." With two more bites it was gone. He took another one.

"Here, Ellen, try one," said Josh. She was just about to peel it when

Pilikia ran over to her and grabbed the banana out of her hand.

"Pilikia, what are you doing?" said Josh. "There are lots to go around. You don't need to take Ellen's."

"Girls can't eat that kind of banana—and the women never eat with the men."

"What?" exclaimed Josh. "Why not? That's the strangest thing I've ever heard."

"It's part of the *kapu*, you know, the rules. The men never eat with the women, and the women don't eat certain foods."

"Why not?" asked Ellen.

"Because that's what the kapu says. Girls can't eat certain kinds of bananas, pork, coconuts, and some fish."

"That stinks," muttered Josh.

"I agree," said Ellen. "That's one of the oddest things I've ever heard. I'm starving—we haven't eaten in over a day—and now you're telling me I can't have a perfectly good banana because of this kapu rule thing?"

Pilikia nodded.

"Are there any other rules we should know about?" asked Will. "I don't want to make a mistake just because I don't know how you do things. That happened to us on some of our other trips. Believe me, it's not good. You don't want that to happen."

"Ellen almost stepped on some sacred temple stairs on our first trip, and she got thrown into jail. Will and I didn't think she'd ever get out," said Josh.

"That wasn't nearly as bad as our third trip when you started mixing up chemicals in Pepik's lab. You're the only person I know who could accidentally invent gunpowder and blow up an entire building," grumbled Will.

"That was cool," agreed Josh, smiling at the memory. "And, for the record, I wasn't breaking any rules doing that. Pepik never said I couldn't mix up that stuff. I was helping him and got a little sidetracked, that's all."

"That may be, but that's not the point. My point is that it definitely wasn't one of your finer moments. You got us into a lot of trouble. I'm surprised we actually made it home alive. I thought we were going to die in Prague."

"Oh, come on. It wasn't that bad," said Josh.

Their little group fell silent as the sound of rushing wind caught their attention. Everyone turned upstream, the direction the wind was coming from. The rush turned into a rumble and then into a roar. Before anyone realized what was happening, a wall of water catapulted down the streambed and surged toward them.

"It's a flash flood!" shouted Pilikia. "Run!"

SIX

PUNISHMENT

Everyone scattered and grabbed onto whatever was handy—tree trunks, branches, stones—and hung on for dear life as the water slammed into them. Josh struggled to keep his head above water. He was so busy trying to stay afloat that he didn't have time to think about Will, Ellen, or Pilikia.

Water surged against him, threatening to pry his fingers from the tree root he was clinging to. Stones and loose branches washed over him, forcing his head under water, but each time he managed to get his head back up and take a deep breath before the next dangerous object was hurled his way.

The water suddenly subsided and vanished almost as quickly as it appeared, fading into a tiny trickle that dribbled down the stream. Josh lay at one side halfway under a tree branch, soaked and exhausted. Once he realized the danger was past, he let go of the root and struggled to his feet. Water poured out of his shorts. All that remained of the flood were the wet pebbles on the bottom of the streambed and the broken branches and leaves on either side.

Josh looked around until he found Will and Ellen. They were safe but soaking wet. "Where's Pilikia? Have you seen her?"

Will and Ellen shook their heads. "We'd better look for her," said Ellen.

"What if she drowned? We'll never find her," moaned Will. "Her body could be miles away by now."

"Will, get a grip," ordered Ellen. "We're fine, and she's probably fine too. We just have to make sure."

Will cleared his throat, setting off a coughing attack. Water dribbled out of his mouth and nose. "Which way should we go?" he croaked.

"Let's follow the path of the water. I'll lead," said Ellen. The three of them hobbled down the damp streambed. There was no sign of Pilikia anywhere.

Josh scanned the rainforest on either side of them. "Where could she be?"

"She could be anywhere. For all we know, the flood sucked her out to sea and we'll never see her again. Then we'll be trapped out here forever. What are we going to do?" whined Will.

"This isn't the time to be thinking about yourself. You should be thinking about Pilikia. Pull yourself together," scolded Ellen.

"I'm serious. If we don't find her, what are we supposed to do? We're not allowed back at her village, not that we could find it on our own, anyway."

"Then we'll pray. We should be doing that anyway."

Here we go again, thought Josh. *She's back on that prayer thing again. We don't need God; we need to make our own plan. All we need to do is find Pilikia. She'll take care of us.* He skidded to a stop when he heard an unfamiliar sound coming from the side of the streambed.

"What?" said Ellen, looking around.

"I think I heard something." Josh waded a few steps into the rainforest undergrowth and disappeared from sight.

Ellen and Will stood staring at the spot where he vanished.

"What should we do?" moaned Will. "Now Josh is gone too."

"Give him a minute. I can hear him thrashing around. Everything's fine."

The two of them jumped at the sound of Josh's voice. "I found her, but she's hurt! Come here, quick!" he shouted.

Will and Ellen crashed through the dense undergrowth until they reached him. Pilikia was sitting on the ground next to a tree stump looking drenched and miserable. A blue bruise was already forming on her forehead and a long gash ran down her right thigh. Every time she glanced down at her leg she turned a little paler.

Ellen bent down beside her. "Ouch! That doesn't look good. Are you okay?"

"I feel fine except for the bump on my head and this stupid cut. It's going to slow me down for days, I just know it." She let out a big sigh. "I should have known that flood was coming."

Josh looked around, astounded that the water was completely gone. "I've never seen anything like this before. Where did all the water go?"

"It's long gone, probably in the ocean by now. That's how a flash flood works: it comes and goes with very little warning. But there were clouds up there earlier." She pointed in the direction of the mountain. "I should have realized it was raining up high."

"Can you walk?" asked Will.

"I'll try. Help me up."

The three siblings carefully helped Pilikia to her feet. Once she was up she took a tentative step forward. She had barely put any weight on her right leg when she gasped. "Ouch … Ouch …" she whimpered, hopping up and down on her good leg, trying to distract herself from the pain.

"I think we've got a problem," muttered Will.

"Imagine that. Thank you for that profound thought of the day," said Ellen.

Will stuck his tongue out at Ellen. "There's no way she can move. What are we supposed to do?"

"You have to help me get back to my village. If we can make it there, my grandmother will spread her special ointment on my cut and bandage it up. I'll be better in no time."

"Aren't you forgetting something?" asked Will.

"What?"

"We're not allowed to go back to your village."

"I'm sure they won't mind if you're helping me. Don't worry; I'll keep you safe," said Pilikia.

"The last time we went into your village things didn't go so well. You should have told them right away that we weren't gods."

"I had a feeling you weren't gods, but I wasn't sure," Pilikia responded wearily. "It doesn't matter. Everything turned out fine."

"Everything turned out fine?" repeated Will. "Your people tried to feed us chewed-up meat and then they got mad at us and banished us to this stupid rainforest and then we were just about killed by a flash flood and you think everything turned out fine? Just so you know, I don't think so." He stood, shaking with anger. "I can't believe you let this happen to us. I'm not taking you back to your village. They don't want us, and we don't want them, either. Make another plan."

Pilikia glared at him. "I made the plan, and I don't care if you like it or not. You don't have a choice. You wouldn't survive in this rain-forest for a day by yourself because you don't know where to go or what to eat. You don't have a choice."

Josh leaned over to his brother. "If I were you, Will, I'd be careful. You don't want to make her mad."

Pilikia pulled her shoulders back and stared at Will defiantly. "It's too late. He already has."

Will furrowed his brow, unsure of what to do. "I'll follow your plan for now, but I'll be watching you. Make one wrong move, and I'll—" A long, fat snake slithered on the ground between them.

"Don't move," commanded Pilikia. "It isn't poisonous, but its bite really stings."

Josh kept an eye on Will, terrified that his brother was going to faint any second. Somehow, Will miraculously managed to summon every ounce of self-control he possessed and held himself together.

"I don't like snakes," whimpered Ellen. "Can someone get it out of here?"

"It'll be gone in a minute if you don't move. You're more interested in it than it is in you," said Pilikia.

They watched the snake slither its way across the path and disappear under a dense bush. "Can we move yet?" asked Will, his voice trembling.

"It should be safe. Go ahead." Pilikia hopped over to Josh and draped her right arm over his shoulders. She used his body to steady herself as they made their way over to the streambed. Will and Ellen followed close behind.

"What are we doing?" asked Will.

"We're following the streambed back to my village. It's a shortcut; it won't take long."

Will pushed his glasses up his nose. "I sure hope she knows what she's doing."

"I guess we'll find out."

Josh's body was aching by the time they reached the outskirts of Pilikia's village. Every time he helped Pilikia take a step, she put all her weight on his shoulders. Even though he was pretty strong, he quickly realized he wasn't used to using his muscles in this way. Will wouldn't have anything to do with Pilikia, so when Josh needed a break Ellen took a turn. She was quite a bit taller than Pilikia, which made things difficult for both of them, so Josh ended up doing most of the work.

"Thanks for your help, Josh," said Pilikia as they made their way down the path.

"Glad to help," he replied through clenched teeth. *I'll be glad when you're back on your own two feet.*

They had just reached the temple when a group of villagers spotted them. One of the men started shouting, motioning wildly at the kids so they would know they weren't allowed back in the village. At that moment an old lady shoved her way through the men and rushed over to Pilikia.

"Oh, Grandma," moaned Pilikia, collapsing into her arms, "I'm glad you're here. Can you fix my leg?"

"Of course, child. Come with me." Pilikia's grandmother lifted her up and effortlessly carried her into the village.

Josh watched them make their way through the crowd, his mouth dangling open. "Wow! I've never seen a grandma do that before," he said. "She must be awfully strong." He, Will, and Ellen stood alone. Most of the villagers moved away, but one or two kept their eyes on them. "What do we do now?" he asked.

"We're not supposed to be here," added Will.

"I know," agreed Ellen, "but I'm scared to go after her. We're not welcome here."

"I'm still hungry," complained Josh, rubbing his belly. "Those bananas were okay, but they were a little green and didn't really fill me up. Do you think we could get some food? Maybe they have some-one like that *almoner* guy we met in England who gave food to people like us."

"I can't believe you're thinking about food at a time like this. You amaze me," said Ellen.

"Thanks," he replied, completely missing her point. "You know, I'm so hungry I'd eat just about anything right about now."

As they stood on the outskirts of the village trying to figure out what to do, one of the priest's assistants came out of the temple and approached them.

"Oh, no, here comes trouble," whispered Will. "We'd better get out of here."

"Just wait." Josh paused. "He doesn't look mad."

"He's not smiling, either."

"That doesn't mean we're in trouble."

"Let's make a run for it," said Will.

Josh grabbed his brother by the arm. "Wait."

The assistant walked over to them. "Pilikia's grandmother asked me to send word that her granddaughter is all right. Pilikia will be up and around within a day or two. She asked me to bring the girl to her." He pointed to Ellen. "The boys are to see Pilikia's father for some food."

"Oh, good. Food!" exclaimed Josh. "Which way do we go?"

The man chuckled. "Follow me. We'll take the girl to Pilikia's hut, then we'll go eat."

"Are you planning on chewing it for us this time?" asked Will, hesitantly.

Ellen whacked him on the arm. "Where are your manners?"

"Sorry," he muttered under his breath.

The man crossed his arms over his chest and gave Will a pained smile. "We only chew foods for the gods. Everyone knows you don't belong in that category." He spun around and marched through the village with the kids trailing behind.

The assistant dropped off Ellen at the hut belonging to Pilikia's family. The boys continued on once she disappeared inside. Josh was fascinated by the activity around him. They passed a hut where canoes were being made, another where the women were cooking, and another where the kids were playing a game like checkers on top of a flat rock. Eventually they reached a second cooking area, one occupied with only men.

Several men were gathered around the *Imu*, ovens formed by lining pits in the ground with rocks. Someone had built a fire on top of each pile of rocks. Josh watched one of the villagers scrape the glowing embers out of one of the pits. Bundles of food wrapped in ginger and banana leaves were placed on top of the stones and then everything was covered with wet leaves, woven mats, and a layer of dirt. Every so often one of the men dribbled water down a bamboo tube into the pit so steam would form, cooking the food.

"Wow. I thought our rice cooker was good, but this is amazing," said Josh. "I wonder how they dreamed this up?"

"I haven't seen any metal here. It's probably the best they could come up with," said Will.

"What do you mean, 'the best they could come up with'? I think they've done a great job. Someone really thought this through. It sure beats cooking over an open fire. The food won't get that smoky taste."

"You're just impressed because you're so hungry," scoffed Will. "I wonder what they're cooking."

Josh cautiously approached a man pouring water down one of the bamboo tubes. "Um, I was wondering, what are you cooking today for dinner?"

The man smiled at him, revealing two rows of perfectly straight white teeth. "I have several bundles in my Imu. Today, we are cooking breadfruit, taro, and dog."

"Dog?" gulped Josh. "Like the four-legged animal, man's best friend?"

"There are many wild dogs on the island, but they're hard to catch. We're always pleased when we get one. It's a nice change from pork and fish."

"Oh," gulped Josh. "I really like dogs. I have a pet dog at home—her name's Finnie. I don't think I could eat one. They cooked a dog for a feast at the last place we stayed," he added, shaking his head. "I couldn't eat it there, either."

"There's fish in the other Imu. We'll find you something to eat," said the man, giving Josh a wink.

"Thanks." Josh jogged back to Will.

"What's on the menu? Anything good?"

"Breadfruit and taro—whatever those are—and dog."

The blood drained from Will's face. "Oh, not again," he groaned.

"Don't worry. He said we could have fish instead."

Will let out a deep breath. "Good. You had me scared for a minute."

When the meal was ready, the men of the village assembled near the Imu, forming a rough line to get their food. Josh was so hungry that he snuck to the front. Will spotted him and hauled him to the back.

"We don't live here. We can't barge up front," said Will.

"I know, but I'm starving. I can't wait," groaned Josh.

Suddenly, all the men straightened up. A tall, fierce-looking man strode into the clearing. He had coffee-colored skin and dark hair and eyes, just like the rest of Pilikia's people, but there was something different about him, something special. He wore a loincloth around his waist and a short cape over his shoulders, revealing his tightly muscled limbs and chest. A whale tooth hung around his neck on a string of braided hair. Everyone grew quiet and watched as he approached Josh and Will.

"I am *Ah-ee-law-nee*, the high chief." His voice was so low it rumbled like thunder. "Pilikia's grandmother tells me that you helped her injured granddaughter return to our village. Thank you."

"No problem. We were glad to help, especially after how badly things went when we first got here," said Josh.

Will kicked Josh in the foot. "Did you have to remind him of that?" he hissed.

"Oops. Sorry."

"I understand there was some confusion about your identity. All is forgotten now. You have redeemed yourselves. You are welcome in our village again."

"Yes!" Josh shouted, pumping his fist into the air. "Thank you!"

"You are most welcome," replied the chief, chuckling. "Follow me, but not too closely. Our food is waiting."

Josh and Will followed the chief to the front of the line. Josh took a huge chunk of fish, some of the strange-looking fruit he had seen in the temple, and a piece of what he believed was taro. Then, following the chief's lead, he sprinkled sea salt on top of it all. The chief added a dollop of *Inamona*, a relish made of roasted nuts, salt, and seaweed. Josh did the same. He and Will followed the chief to a nearby tree. The chief motioned for them to sit down next to the tree trunk. Once they were settled, he sat down a little way away. Josh placed his plate on his lap, careful not to tip his huge stack of food. Will's task was much simpler; all he had on his plate was a thin piece of fish. Josh waited for the chief to begin eating and then he began tucking into his own dinner.

"So, how come you get to be chief?" he asked through a mouthful of food.

Will glared at him. "Don't ask stupid questions and don't talk with your mouth full."

Josh made a rude face back. "I can ask the chief whatever I want. It's none of your business."

The chief lowered his plate to his lap. "The men of my family have been chiefs in this village for generations. *Mana* flows from my ancestors into me, giving me power and wisdom to rule over my people."

"What's mana?" interrupted Josh.

The chief raised his eyebrows slightly. "Mana is the power that we find within ourselves. It comes to us in two ways: through the power that resided in our ancestors, which is passed on to the next generation, and through our personal accomplishments and talents. The greater your mana, the greater your position in your family and in your village, and the greater the burden you have for others."

"So, having a lot of mana isn't always a good thing," noted Josh.

"It is if you honor the responsibility that goes with it."

"I wouldn't want to look after everyone else. I have enough trouble looking after myself."

"You got that right," muttered Will under his breath.

The chief raised his eyebrows. "It must be different where you come from. Here on our island we look after one another first. The good of the clan is more important than the good of any one person. We strive for everyone to be happy, not just ourselves. The *we* comes before *me*."

"Hmm." Josh scratched his chin. "That sounds like a good thing. It sounds like something I might have learned in Sunday school, you know, the idea of putting others before yourself. It's just that if I did that, I might not get the things I want. That would be hard." He scooped the last bit of food off his plate with his fingers and shoved it into his mouth.

The chief gave him a strained smile. "In our village the younger people always defer to the older people as well as their parents. You definitely wouldn't always get what you wanted."

Josh uncrossed his legs and tried to stand up, but it was awkward as his left leg had fallen asleep. He limped over to the chief, shaking his leg to try and get the feeling back. Josh stood only a few steps away from the chief when the older man held up his hand.

"What are you doing?" he growled.

"I thought I'd come sit beside you so we wouldn't have to shout at each other."

"You can't come near me," said the chief. His hand hung in the air, unwavering.

"Why not? We were having such a nice talk. I like learning about your village. It's interesting."

"You have less mana than I do, and I don't want to lose any of mine to you."

"What? I don't understand this mana stuff. You don't need to worry—I definitely don't want any of yours. I promise I won't take any of it."

"Mana is a fragile thing. It can transfer from a chief to a commoner like you if the commoner gets too close."

Josh took a step forward. "What do you mean 'commoner'? I'm no commoner."

Will began waving his arms in an effort to get Josh's attention. When Josh finally looked his way, Will made a slicing motion across his neck. Josh ignored his suggestion to be quiet.

"For your information, I ate with a lord and his family in England, and he was so impressed with me that he practically adopted me into his family. He gave us sets of armor and huge swords with jewels in their handles. We're practically royalty, you know. That's probably why you guys thought we were gods when we first arrived."

Will rushed over, grabbed Josh by the arm, and dragged him away from the chief. "What are you thinking? I can't believe you talked to the chief like that. You're going to get us into more trouble."

"I was just trying to explain things to him. He obviously has no clue who we are," sulked Josh.

"As far as he's concerned we're nobodies, and that's fine with me. You don't have to be the most important person all of the time."

"But I *am* important."

"You're not nearly as important as you like to think you are."

The boys fell silent when the chief stood up. "Young man," the chief said, his voice booming across the eating area as he stared at Josh, "You are rude, boorish, and disrespectful. If everyone in my village behaved as badly as you just did, our lives would be chaos. The reason our village has prospered is because we take care of each other. We don't demand our own rights at the expense of others. We punish people like you who exhibit bad-mannered, self-serving attitudes."

"Punish?" gulped Josh.

"Yes, punish."

"I wasn't trying to be rude, honest. I just wanted you to know that I'm important too."

"That's exactly the problem. In our village, children know their place. They don't talk back to their elders. I hereby order you banished from this village until the time of the next full moon."

"But I was just kidding! I didn't mean to sound rude. You're right, I'm not that important after all. You're the main guy, and I'm okay with that." Josh looked to Will for reassurance, but he didn't find any. All the blood had drained from Will's face, and he was swallowing repeatedly so he wouldn't throw up.

"My punishment has been given. The people of this village will not talk to you, feed you, show you where to sleep, or help you in any way. You are on your own."

Josh's stomach heaved. "But what about my brother and sister? Can I talk to them? Please?"

"You may speak with them before you leave, but only briefly, and they will not be allowed to help you in any way."

Josh looked at Will. "When's the next full moon?"

Will gulped. "It was hard to see the moon last night, but I think it was almost full. Hopefully, it will only be a few days." He tried to put on a brave front for Josh's sake but didn't quite succeed. His chin quivered as he continued. "You'll be fine. You're braver than most people I know." Will lowered his voice so only Josh could hear. "Stay close to the village just in case we need you, okay?"

"I'll try," sniffled Josh, his eyes filling with tears. He turned and walked slowly out of the village, away from the chief and Will and Pilikia and Ellen, and disappeared into the rainforest.

— SEVEN —

THE PERFECT DAY

❀▩❀▩❀▩❀▩❀▩❀▩❀▩❀

Josh stumbled down the trail he had taken earlier through the rain-forest until he was a little way away, far enough to please the chief, but close enough that Will and Ellen could find him in case of an emergency. He sank down under a fern that bordered the path, feeling exhausted and sorry for himself.

Why did that chief have to be so mean? All I was trying to do was tell him how important we are—we usually help the people in the places we visit—but he didn't get it. I wish I had some of that gunpowder I made in Prague. That would get his attention. He smiled at the thought, imagining how surprised everyone would be if he created an explosion in the village.

Josh looked around, taking in the shadowy greenery around him. As he realized how alone he was, Josh's heart sank. *Maybe I should have listened to Will. He wanted me to be quiet, and I ignored him. Why does he have to be right all of the time?* He let out a big sigh. *I wonder what Ellen's doing. I hate it when the three of us are apart—it doesn't feel right. Pilikia's probably all bandaged up by now, and I bet they're doing all sorts of fun things together.* Just then he remembered that Pilikia had promised to take him to all her favorite places. *Now she's probably going to take Ellen instead of me, and I'll miss all the fun. Why did I have to get into trouble today?*

A tear dribbled down his cheek. He wiped it away, stretched out on his back, and closed his eyes.

Josh woke up when he heard the sound of voices. He rubbed his eyes, struggling to get his bearings. The forest was dim in the fading light of evening. All he could see was a curtain of green above and around him. He leaned forward, straining to catch what was being said.

"Why didn't you go after him?" said Ellen. "He shouldn't be out here all by himself. Remember that huge snake? It could be dangerous."

"I couldn't exactly leave with the chief standing right there. You should have seen him, Ellen. I didn't know Josh could be that rude. He was out of control. He kept telling the chief how important he was. Josh said he was practically royalty because of our trip to England. They don't care about his armor or the sword Lord Richard gave him, just like they don't care that we time traveled here or that we know all kinds of things they haven't even thought of yet. I just don't understand why Josh would be so selfish."

Will continued walking until he was next to Josh's hiding spot. "I tried to stop him, but he didn't listen. I've never seen him be such a brat before. Mom and Dad would have been furious if they saw how he was behaving."

Josh scooted back. Hot tears poured down his face. *It wasn't my fault. The chief had it in for me. No one's on my side.*

"What should we do now?" he heard Ellen say. She called out his name three times. He didn't respond. "He shouldn't be out here alone, especially at night."

"We shouldn't be, either," added Will. "The chief said we were supposed to stay away from him."

"I just need to know that he's okay. Then we can go back to the village."

"Come on, Josh, we know you're out there," called Will. "What if he's lost? We'll never find him." His voice grew more panicky. "What if the time stone won't reappear unless we're all together? I bet that's how it works. We've always been together when it comes. Why does that exasperating brother of ours always have to wreck everything?

"Come on, Josh. We know you're out here," he hollered again. "We can't help you if we can't find you."

"I don't want your help," Josh whispered. He listened to Ellen work her way through the underbrush until she was almost at the spot where he was hiding.

"Come on, Josh. We know you're here. Come out," she shouted.

Josh held his breath and sat absolutely still. A few minutes later he heard Will and Ellen move away, their voices fading as they walked back to the village. In the sudden silence, Josh felt a wave of discouragement, but he was too exhausted to cry. Once again he stretched out beneath the ferns, closed his eyes, and fell asleep.

Bright morning sunlight filtered down through the trees as Josh crawled out from under his fern shelter. He blinked, stretched, and wandered around until he found a path. As he traveled through the rainforest, he tried to memorize some details so he wouldn't get lost. After five minutes of trying, he gave up; everything looked the same.

"At least it's safe out here," he said aloud. "I haven't seen any wild animals except for that big snake yesterday. I wonder if they have wild pigs out here. If I see any, I'll grab a vine and swing over them just like I did in the jungle with Puma. I'm good at this jungle stuff."

He continued down the path, whistling "O Come All Ye Faithful" without even realizing it. The rustle of a nearby fern caught his eye. He stopped and stared at the spot. The fern was still for a second, then moved again.

Josh's eyes grew wide. "I bet it's one of those wild pigs," he whispered. He looked around to find the nearest vine, but before he could find one the fern moved to one side.

Josh ducked into the brush. The rustling came closer. He hunched over, making himself as small as possible. The rustling became louder and louder. When it was right beside him, it stopped.

Oh, no, I'm dead. I'd better make a run for it. He sprang to his feet and took a gigantic leap, landing a meter away in a pile of fresh animal dung.

Pilikia popped out from behind a nearby fern, spotted Josh, and burst out laughing.

"What are you doing here?" squealed Josh. "Was that noise from you?"

"You have to watch where you land out here." Pilikia grabbed Josh's hand and pulled him to his feet. He stood in front of her, scowling.

"Why'd you have to trick me like that? That was mean. Besides, aren't you supposed to be at home, resting?"

Pilikia pointed to her bandaged leg. "My grandmother patched me up. I'm as good as new. Once Grandmother cleaned the cut we realized it wasn't nearly as bad as it looked."

"At least you're feeling better. That's good."

Pilikia returned his smile. "Want to go exploring?"

"That sounds good to me. Let's get out of here."

The two of them skipped down the trail, stomping on ferns and other low-growing plants. Their first stop was a grove of coconut trees.

"Have you ever tried coconut milk before?" asked Pilikia.

Josh shook his head.

"Want to try some?"

"I don't know. Does it taste good?"

"Of course!"

"Okay. How do we get the coconuts?"

Pilikia looked up. Josh followed her gaze, scanning the treetops until he spotted several round green coconuts at the top of one of the trees. "How are we supposed to get up there?"

"Like this." Pilikia placed her hands on either side of the smooth, narrow trunk and scurried up to the top. Josh watched in fascination at how efficiently she moved. "Come on, it's your turn," she shouted from her perch just below the coconuts.

Josh put his hands on either side of the tree trunk next to hers and tried to pull himself up. He was used to climbing trees—he did it all the time at home—but this one had no branches to hold on to. He pulled as hard as he could with his arms, but he was barely able to lift his body off the ground. He rested for a minute, firmly gripping onto the trunk so he wouldn't slip back down, and then he repeated the process again, moving up another few centimeters.

"Come on, Josh, you can do it," shouted Pilikia.

"This is hard work," he muttered, wiping the sweat off his brow. "I'm not sure I can make it to the top."

"You can do it, I know you can. It will all be worth it when you taste that coconut milk. It tastes much better when you pick the coconut yourself."

"I sure hope you're right." Josh grabbed a new section of the trunk and pulled himself up, using the inside of his legs and his feet to support some of his weight. Before long, he was high above the ground, about two-thirds of the way up the tree.

He looked around, astonished by the view beneath him. The rainforest was on his left, running down a long, narrow valley on one side of the mountain. On his right was more arid land. There were still bunches of trees, but they weren't as lush as the rainforest growth. Large expanses of rocks and sand separated the patches of green. In the distance, just past the rock and sand, the landscape was barren, the ground black. It reminded him of pictures he'd seen of the surface of the moon. Beyond that the deep blue expanse of the ocean rolled out endlessly.

"What's taking you so long?" shouted Pilikia. "Are you scared to climb to the top?"

"Me, scared?" he replied indignantly. "I was just looking around. What a great view."

"I suppose," she shouted, rolling her eyes. "We've got lots to do. Get moving."

"Yes, boss." Josh gave her a salute.

"What does that mean?"

"Oh, never mind." He continued scrambling his way up, taking care to grip the trunk extra tight. It was a long way down to the ground. Josh was just below Pilikia when the bark became even smoother. No matter how he tried, he couldn't climb any farther. Every time he pulled himself up he began to slide back down.

"Try harder," yelled Pilikia. "You can do it."

Josh shook his head; his arms and legs were tired. He grabbed the trunk and made one final attempt to pull himself up. It didn't work. He began sliding down, unable to stop. He had picked up speed by the time he reached the rougher bark and realized he was out of control, but he didn't know what to do about it. Pain wracked his legs and arms as he clung to the tree, desperately trying to slow his descent. When he was almost at the bottom, he loosened his grip. A feeling of relief flooded his body as his limbs shifted away from the coarse bark. It was canceled a second later by the pain of landing unceremoniously on his back.

Josh lay there, dazed, as Pilikia walked over carrying two large coconuts. He hadn't even noticed her climb down. He groaned as he sat up, the skin on his arms and legs raw and burning. Pilikia handed him a coconut. "That was a good try. Here, have one of mine."

Josh shook it; he could hear some liquid sloshing around inside. "How do you get the milk out?"

"You have to make a hole in it. Then you can drink the milk and eat the nut meat inside." She grabbed a sharp stone lying on the ground and struck the coconut with a practiced hand until a jagged crack appeared in its side. She quickly lifted it to her lips and sucked the liquid out. "Mmm, that was good; it's perfectly ripe." Pilikia handed Josh her rock. "Here, open yours."

Josh gave her a curious look. "I thought you weren't allowed to eat with me."

Pilikia's hand flew up to her mouth. "Oh, you're right. I was so busy having fun I completely forgot about the kapu."

"What are we supposed to do now?"

There was a long silence as Pilikia considered her options. "I already broke the kapu—I can't fix that. I've never done that before. Don't tell anyone, okay?"

"Your secret is safe with me."

"Good. Let's open your coconut."

Josh smashed the rock against the side of his coconut. It glanced off, almost striking his leg. He concentrated harder, hammering it again and again. Nothing happened. "This isn't working," he grumbled. He lifted the coconut above his head and threw it onto the ground. It still didn't break.

"I wouldn't do that if I were you," said Pilikia.

"Well, you're not me. I think this works better." He repeated the motion, throwing the coconut over and over again until it shattered into many small pieces.

"Quick, grab them," said Pilikia. She handed him one of the bigger pieces that had a thin film of coconut milk inside. "Here, drink this."

Josh took a slurp of the coconut milk. It was thin and clear, not at all like the milk he was used to. "Yuck! This stuff tastes terrible."

"Try the meat." Pilikia handed him another piece of the shell lined with coconut meat.

"How do you eat the white stuff without getting the shell?"

"You scrape it off with your teeth." Josh watched as Pilikia lifted the shell to her mouth and scraped it clean.

Josh tried to do the same. It wasn't as simple as it looked. Eventually he gave up and scraped away at the shell with his fingernail. Once he had a reasonably sized pile of shavings he popped them into his mouth. "You sure have to go to a lot of trouble just to eat a little coconut," he observed.

"If you were better at it you wouldn't think it was so much work. What should we do now?"

"I'd like to go swimming in the ocean. How far is it from here?"

"It's just a little walk. If we hurry, we can do some surfing."

Josh stared at her, wide eyed. "You know how to surf?"

"Of course. Everyone here knows how to surf. My people have been doing it for generations."

"Really?" said Josh, still surprised.

"Of course. You sure ask some strange questions."

Josh jumped to his feet. He winced as he moved—his skin was still raw—but he was so excited that he overlooked the pain. "What are we waiting for? Let's go!"

The two of them ran through the rainforest. Josh tried to ignore the painful scrapes on his legs. Pilikia's wound didn't seem to slow her down. Their journey was easier once they left the forest for the barren plain. Josh found himself dodging boulders instead of ferns. The sun beat down on him, forcing his body to produce buckets of sweat to cool him off, but he was so excited he didn't care.

Suddenly, Pilikia veered off to the right and ducked into a tunnel. Josh scurried in behind her. It was difficult moving from the bright sun into the dark cave. Unable to see, he stumbled along, trying to get his bearings. Once his eyes had adjusted, he could see that the tunnel was almost perfectly round and about twice as tall as he was. It had a stale, waterlogged smell to it. Straggly vines broke through the rough walls every few feet and water dripped from the ceiling, forming shallow puddles on the floor.

"Where are we?" asked Josh, uneasily.

"We're in an old lava tube. It's a shortcut to the ocean," said Pilikia.

"How did it get here?"

"It formed a long time ago when lava ran underground through it."

"Have you seen lava in here before?"

"No, silly. It happened a long time ago, long before my grandmother was born. It's perfectly safe."

"Whew," said Josh. "You had me worried there for a minute." He wiggled his shoulders back and forth, trying to drive out the chill that had settled in his spine. "It's dark in here. Let's keep moving."

They made their way down the tube. It became so dark that Josh couldn't see a thing. He held his hand out in front of his face and panicked when he discovered he couldn't even see his own body. Pilikia grabbed him by the arm, startling him, and guided him along.

After a few minutes the tunnel slowly grew brighter. Josh spotted an opening as they rounded a corner. The two of them sprinted down the last section and jumped out onto a beautiful black sand beach. Sheer black cliffs bordered the sides of the small cove and gentle waves lapped against the shoreline. The contrast between the black sand and the brilliant blue water was startling.

Josh bent down and scooped up a handful of sand. It was far coarser than normal sand. He smiled as he watched it trickle between his fingers. "I've never seen sand like this before. This is amazing."

"It comes from the volcanic rock," explained Pilikia, pointing to the clumps of jagged rock jutting out of the surf. "The waves beat against it, day in, day out, and before long you have black sand."

"I wish we had sand like this where I live." Josh looked out at the ocean. The water within the cove was calm, but just past the confines of the beach the white-tipped waves were much larger and dangerous looking. "Are you sure it's safe to surf here?"

"Of course. I come here all the time."

"What are we surfing on?"

Pilikia ran to the back part of the beach and returned carrying two surfboards. "You get the little one," she said, dropping the shorter one at Josh's feet. "It's for beginners."

Josh inspected his board. It looked a lot like the belly board he liked to use at the beach at home, except it was made of wood instead of Styrofoam. It was about two-thirds of his height—much smaller than the board Pilikia held at her side—and was covered with scratches and dents.

Josh glanced over at Pilikia's board. It was longer than his and much nicer. Her board was made of *wili wili*, a tree that grew all over the island, and it had been polished to a glossy shine.

"That's a nice board. Where did you get it?"

"One of the men in the village made it for me. He made it thinner than most so it isn't so heavy for me to carry."

"How come it's so shiny?"

"I take good care of it. I always dry it when I'm done, and I oil it so it stays nice and shiny." She shifted the board to her side and ran headlong into the surf.

A minute later Pilikia was lying on her board, paddling out into the surf. Josh didn't move from his spot on the beach. He ran his hand down his board, fingering the well-worn wood, wondering how it could possibly float let alone hold him up.

"Come on," yelled Pilikia. "What are you waiting for? Let's go!"

"Okay. Here goes nothing." Josh tucked the board under his arm, sprinted down the beach, and plunged into the water.

EIGHT

RED-HOT LAVA

🌞🔲🌞🔲🌞🔲🌞🔲🌞🔲🌞🔲🌞

Josh's surfboard popped up to the surface of the water. He wiggled back and forth until he was lying comfortably across it and paddled after Pilikia. As they approached the edge of the cove where the calm water met the rough surf, Pilikia gave Josh's board a big push, sending him back toward the beach.

"Hey, what do you think you're doing?" he shouted. "I'm coming with you."

"You have to practice on the little waves first. Try riding them to the shore. You need to be able to stand on your board and ride those waves first. Once you've mastered them, you can come out with me."

Josh reluctantly turned his board around and relaxed as the waves carried him to shore. Every few minutes he looked back. Pilikia was paddling out, her body appearing smaller and smaller. *I sure hope she knows what she's doing.*

When he reached the beach, Josh dropped his surfboard onto the sand and sat down at the water's edge. It was midday—the sun was high in the sky—so without sunglasses he had to squint to see his friend. He eventually spotted Pilikia way out, shuttling back and forth as she tried to find the perfect wave. Suddenly, she paddled furiously toward a large one and caught it just as it was rising into the air.

Josh watched spellbound as Pilikia rode the wave, her arms extended on either side of her. The wave grew bigger and bigger as it moved toward the beach, carrying her along at an incredible speed.

Suddenly, Pilikia faltered—it looked like she was going to fall off her board. Josh clenched his fists and held his breath. He let out a big sigh when she regained her balance and continued zooming toward him.

The waves slowed when she passed the outer edge of the cove, but she remained upright until her board washed onto the sand. Pilikia wiped the salt water out of her eyes and let out a loud whoop. "Did you see that? That was amazing!" She leaned over and gave Josh a wet hug. "I'm so glad we came here today. How did you do?"

"I felt like I was on a kiddie ride at a carnival, like the ladybug ride or one of those little trains. They're fun when you're two, but they're lousy when you're twelve."

Pilikia frowned at him. "What are a ladybug ride and a train?"

"Oh, never mind. It's too hard to explain. I want to go out in the big waves with you. It's no fun here by the shore."

"Did you practice like I told you to?"

Josh's mouth twitched back and forth as he contemplated his answer. "Sort of."

"Are you a good swimmer?"

"Of course." He gave her a crooked smile. "I haven't drowned, yet."

"I have to warn you, you're on your own once we're past the cove."

Josh jumped to his feet and grabbed his board. "No problem. I'll be fine. Let's go!"

The two of them paddled out together, Pilikia crouched on her board and Josh lying across his. Josh's heart began beating faster as they left the calm water of the cove. He looked back over his shoulder. The beach seemed like it was a million miles away. Maybe this wasn't such a good idea after all. Each new swell lifted him up high before plummeting him back down into the troughs between the waves. It was far scarier than he had expected. His stomach churned as he watched the ocean roll around him.

"Do you think I should go back?" he shouted. Pilikia couldn't hear him. Just then, she spotted the wave she wanted and motioned for Josh to join her. He struggled to pull his knees onto his board—by now he was shaking so badly that he could barely control his movements. Just as he paddled over to her, Josh felt a wave rise up beneath him. Before he knew what was happening, he was riding the slope of the wave, hanging onto the sides of his surfboard for dear life.

"Stand up," shouted Pilikia.

Josh struggled to his feet, his legs trembling, still holding onto the sides of his board. He looked up and saw Pilikia gracefully surfing along, beaming with delight. "I can do this too," he said. "There's no way I'm letting a girl outsurf me."

He let go of the sides of his board with one hand, then the other, and slowly straightened his back until he was standing up. His surfboard wobbled back and forth beneath him, but he managed to keep his balance.

Josh glanced over at Pilikia again. She was doing a little dance on her board, her arms and hips waving as she flew toward the shore. Josh got a little bolder and lifted his arms straight up in the air. The movement threw him off balance. He hung there for a moment, unsure of what to do. Before he figured it out, he felt himself falling and he plunged headfirst into the curl of the wave.

Everything happened so fast that he didn't get time to take a breath before the wave forced him deep below the surface. His eyes burned as he looked through the crystal blue water around him. Once he had his bearings he paddled up, his lungs burning, and took a huge gulp of air as he broke through the surface. Josh sank back into the water and swam a few strokes on his side. Confident he was safe, he looked around. He had floated into the quiet water of the cove. Pilikia was gliding up to the beach, his surfboard drifting in behind her.

He kept swimming until he reached the shore, his shoulders aching, not stopping until he could touch the bottom. He stood up, still wobbly, and walked the last few steps to shore before collapsing onto the sand.

Pilikia rushed over to him. "Are you okay?"

"That was not a good idea. I don't feel so good," he said, rubbing his head as he slowly sat up. "Do you think we could head back to the village?" He paused. "Oh, that's right; I can't go back. The chief kicked me out."

"I heard you were rude to him. That's one thing you should never do—we always show respect to our elders."

"I know that now. I won't make that mistake again."

"Did he say when you could come back?"

"I think he said not until the new moon, whenever that is."

"Wow. I'm surprised. That's in about two weeks."

"Two weeks! You've got to be kidding. Will said it would be sooner than that. I can't wait that long. We probably won't even be here then. Our trips usually last just a few days." Josh let out a big sigh and fell back onto the sand. "Will and Ellen are going to hate me."

"I'll look after you if you want." She gave him a hopeful smile.

"But I thought everyone from the village was supposed to avoid me."

She shrugged her shoulders. "We're friends, remember?" Josh rolled over and held out his fist. They did their secret handshake, followed by a weak shout of "friends." Josh was too sore to do it with any enthusiasm.

"Do you want me to bring you some food and help you find a place to sleep?" asked Pilikia.

"Isn't that breaking the rules?"

"The rules don't apply to people who know how to get around them."

Josh lowered his eyebrows. "Did you just say what I think you just said?"

She nodded. "I already broke one rule today. What's a few more?"

He grinned from ear to ear. "Now you're talking my language."

"Come on," said Pilikia, rising to her feet. She offered him her hand. He took it and pulled himself up. "Let's head back."

Pilikia led Josh back toward the village along a different route. They took a rest break at a waterfall and enjoyed a swim in one of its three freshwater pools. Pilikia picked some fruit and ate it sitting next to Josh, even though she was breaking the kapu again. They climbed trees, dashed along overgrown trails, and inspected a spider web as tall as they were.

Feeling thirsty, they stopped at a mountain stream for a drink. Josh looked over at Pilikia, water dripping down his chin, and smiled. "I wish this day would never end. It's been one of the best days of my life. You're a great pal—you're like a sister, only better." He put out his hand and they did their secret handshake again, this time with more enthusiasm.

"It's great we like the same things, isn't it?" asked Pilikia.

"It sure is, except for surfing. I don't know if I'd try that again."

"It was your idea to come out deep with me. I warned you."

"I know," replied Josh with a sheepish grin.

They were almost back at the village when they came across a big tree that blocked the path, splitting it in two. Pilikia turned left and walked past it. Josh stopped in front of the tree and looked around.

Pilikia had taken about twenty steps down the path before she realized Josh wasn't with her. "Come on, we're almost there," she shouted.

Josh didn't move. "Where does this other path go?" he asked, pointing to the right of the tree.

Pilikia ran back up to the path and rejoined him. "It goes to the City of Refuge. You don't want to go there. Come on, let's get moving."

"What's the City of Refuge?"

"People who break the kapu go there. A priest performs a special ceremony so they'll be forgiven for whatever they did wrong. That way they can return home without being punished."

"Why is the path grown in?"

"It's not used very much. Most of the people in my village keep the kapu. Everyone, that is, except for you."

"And you," said Josh, pointing his finger at her. "You broke the kapu when you ate with me today. Does that mean you have to go there?"

"No. I'd have to do something way worse than eat with you. But don't tell anyone I did that, okay?"

"Should I have gone to the City of Refuge after I talked back to the chief?"

"No. That's not bad enough either. You got off easy because you didn't do something really bad."

"You call this easy?" exclaimed Josh. "You've got to be kidding. Being sent away for two weeks is not easy. Maybe I would have been better off at that refuge place. At least I'd have someone to take care of me."

"You're better off to wait it out—it's safer. Besides, the only people who go to the City of Refuge are the ones who've done really bad things, like killing someone. If you kill someone, that person's relatives can kill you in return as punishment. The only way you can escape is if you can get to the City of Refuge before they do. They would probably chase you all the way there. If they catch you before you get through the gate, they can kill you without being punished themselves."

"That sounds scary," said Josh. "I hope I never have to go there."

Pilikia turned and started down the left path again. "Don't do anything dumb and you won't."

"Thanks for the advice." Josh meandered down the path after her.

As they approached the village, Josh spotted Ellen and Will walking down the path toward them—and they saw him. Ellen squealed with delight and gave Josh a hug so big she lifted his feet right off the ground. Will hung back and glared.

"Where have you been?" asked Ellen, breathlessly. "We've been looking all over for you."

"I know," said Josh. "Pilikia was showing me around. She took me to some amazing places. Maybe we can all go tomorrow."

"Just a minute," interrupted Will. His eyes narrowed. "How did you know we were looking for you?"

Josh grinned sheepishly. "I heard you calling me last night, but I was mad so I stayed hiding."

"We've been looking for you all day. Ellen and I walked for miles, calling for you until we were hoarse. We were really worried. I can't believe you'd hide from us on purpose. Why do you always have to be so difficult?"

"I wasn't trying to be difficult. I just didn't feel like coming out. I knew you were mad at me."

"You got that right. We are."

"That was pretty inconsiderate," added Ellen.

Will nodded. "Don't ever do that to us again."

"Okay. If I ever hear you looking for me again I promise I'll tell you where I am, unless we're playing hide-and-seek or something."

"It's a deal." Ellen gave Josh another hug. "I'm so glad we're back together."

"Me, too," said Josh, "but I can't go back to the village, remember? Pilikia said it will take two weeks before the new moon comes out. I can't go back until then."

"The chief said *full* moon, not *new* moon," corrected Will. "I saw the moon last night. It looked almost full to me. It's not going to take two weeks. It might even be a full moon tomorrow."

"That's great," exclaimed Pilikia. "You'll be allowed back in the village before you know it."

"Good. So, what's the plan?" asked Josh.

"We'd better head back to the village. Night will be here soon.

I'll get Josh some food and help him find a place to sleep." Pilikia glanced at Ellen and Will. "Don't tell anyone I spent the day with him, okay?"

Ellen and Will gave each other a knowing look. "We'll talk about it later," said Ellen.

Pilikia led the three of them up the final stretch of the path. The closer they got to the village, the wider the path became. They passed the patches of breadfruit and taro, groves of banana and coconut trees, and pens of chicken and pigs.

They were just a minute away when Pilikia stopped and showed Josh a hiding spot in the bushes along the path. He pushed his way through the leaves until he reached a little clearing. As he sat cross-legged on the ground, his eyes began to burn and he started to cough. "Pilikia, don't go yet. Something smells really bad in here. Are you sure this is where I'm supposed to be?"

Pilikia, Will, and Ellen made their way over to him. "Yuck! It smells like rotten eggs," said Ellen, plugging her nose. "Where's it coming from?"

"Maybe they have those smelly plants like the one we saw in the Mayan jungle. It smelled like this," said Josh.

"No, this is way worse." Will circled the clearing, pushing the plants to one side so he could peer over them. "Guys, come here, quick! There's something strange happening."

Everyone rushed over. A greenish puddle had formed just behind the clearing. Steam rose from it as it bubbled, filling the air with a horrible smell. The leaves around the puddle had lost their color, turning a sickly shade of yellow.

"What on earth is that? It looks like toxic waste," said Ellen.

"It's gas from the volcano. It usually smells bad," said Pilikia.

"Volcanic gas?" exclaimed Will. "See! I told you the volcano is ready to erupt. Here's your proof."

"Calm down. Just because there's a stinky puddle in the middle of the rainforest doesn't mean that the volcano is about to erupt. You're jumping to some awfully big conclusions," said Ellen.

"I agree." Josh put his hands on his hips and looked Will straight in the eye. "I've been all over this island today, and I didn't see anything like this. It's probably a freak thing that only happens once in a while."

Will crossed his arms and swallowed repeatedly. "You don't know anything about volcanoes."

Josh stuck out his tongue. "You don't know as much as you think you know, Mr. Volcano Expert."

"This is my island," interrupted Pilikia, "and I know a lot about volcanoes. I already told you Pele hasn't erupted in a long time. We have nothing to worry about. Every so often we see a puddle like this, but nothing else happens."

"Are you sure?" squeaked Will.

"Positive," she replied. "Josh, you wait here. We'll get you some food."

"Sounds good to me. Just make sure it's not dog meat, okay?"

The three of them had been gone less than a minute when Josh heard Will scream. He ran out of his clearing and sprinted down the path after them. Will was so upset he was jumping up and down.

Josh pushed his way past him. He stopped dead in his tracks when he spotted hot lava bubbling across the path, slowly moving toward them like thick orange paint. The top of the flow had hardened, forming a black crust, but the outer edges were still red-hot. The lava devoured everything it touched.

"I told you that volcano was going to blow!" shrieked Will. "You aren't going to get better proof than this."

Ellen grabbed him by the arm. "Calm down. You're acting hysterical. Pilikia, have you ever seen lava like this before?"

Pilikia shook her head.

Josh glanced over at Will again. His brother's reaction had left him shaken. "I agree with Will," he said. "I think we're in big trouble."

— NINE —

MORE TROUBLE

◯▨◯▨◯▨◯▨◯▨◯▨◯

ou're overreacting," insisted Pilikia. "Just because there's lava on the path doesn't mean the volcano's going to erupt."

"No offense, Pilikia, but I hardly think you're an expert in this department. Is there someone in your village we can talk to?" asked Ellen.

"A geologist would be good," said Josh.

"A volcanologist would be even better," added Will.

"We could try and talk with the chief, but we need to be careful how we approach him. Josh knows that better than anyone," said Pilikia.

"She's right," agreed Josh. "I'm not going anywhere near him. If he gets mad at me again, I might have to go to the City of Refuge, and I'm not sure I want to go there."

"Where's that?" asked Ellen.

"I'll tell you later."

The eerie sound of a conch horn interrupted their discussion. It sputtered at first, but then it grew loud and strong. The noise had barely tapered off when it started again. After three long blows it fell silent.

"What was that?" said Ellen.

"That means the *ali'i*, the king, is here. I wonder if anyone knew he was coming. We haven't seen him in a long time. Everyone in my village will be preoccupied with his visit."

"But we need to speak to the chief about this lava," insisted Will. "It can't wait. What if more is coming?"

"You're right. We have to do something. Follow me through the village."

"Do you have a plan?" asked Josh.

"We'll make it up as we go," said Pilikia.

They reached the village just in time to see the king and the chief approach the temple, followed by a handful of servants. The king looked like the chief, but he appeared to be at least twenty years older. Everyone from the village had turned up to see him, but the villagers hung back, careful to keep their distance. The priest greeted the two leaders at the temple door, bowing low, and then the three of them entered the temple.

"Oh no, we're too late. They'll be in there for hours," moaned Pilikia.

"We can't wait. What if more lava is on the way?" said Will.

"Will's right. We have to do something. One of us has to talk to the chief and the king." Ellen looked at Will expectantly.

"I think it should be Josh," said Will.

"No, thanks." Josh took a step back. "Anyone can do it. Why me?"

"You're the bravest person here. I think it makes sense that you'd talk to him." Will gave his brother a hopeful smile.

"Okay, fine. I'll go." He started walking toward the temple.

Ellen grabbed his arm and tried to pull him back. "What are you doing? You can't go in there. You've been in enough trouble already."

Josh jerked his arm away. "There's no point in getting you guys into trouble. How much worse can it get for me, anyway?"

"A lot worse," said Pilikia, grabbing his other arm. "You need to think about this. You can't just barge in without a plan."

Josh pulled away from her, too. "I have a plan. Just watch. I'll be right back."

He marched over to the temple, through the gate, past the guards standing at the base of the stairs. Before they realized what was happening, he'd scampered up the steps into the building. He immediately spotted the priest—the priest was handing a rotten pig to the king who was standing in front of the five wooden statues. The priest's assistants stood a distance away, waiting for further instructions.

Josh could hear their voices, but he couldn't understand anything they were saying. Doubt washed over him. *What was I thinking? I can't go talk to these people. They'll kill me.* He stood for a second, considering his options. *I can't go back to the others either. If we don't tell the chief about the lava, the whole village could be destroyed. What should I do?*

He hesitated for a moment before taking a step forward and then another and another. It felt like his feet were moving by a power other than his own. In just seconds he slipped between the king's bodyguards and scurried over to the king.

"Um, excuse me, sir, I mean, your kingship." The king turned around. He was tall and muscular with a full head of thick dark hair. Years of exposure to the sun had given him deep wrinkles, but they only enhanced his regal bearing. He was dressed in a loincloth and a beautiful feathered cape. A fancy charm dangled from a braided cord around his neck.

"What are you doing here?" asked the king, his perfectly spaced teeth flashing as he spoke. He handed the pig to the priest. "Commoners are not allowed in the *heuka*."

One of the priest's assistants grabbed Josh by the shoulders and led him away. "You've caused enough trouble. Get out of here before they punish you further," he hissed.

"But I need to speak with the chief and the king," said Josh, his voice raised. "It's important."

"Not as important as their meeting," replied the assistant. He shoved Josh toward the doorway. "Be on your way."

Josh gritted his teeth. "I'm not leaving until I talk with them."

The assistant crossed his arms. "Oh, yes, you are. You're leaving right now." He nodded for the king's bodyguards to remove Josh.

Josh lunged past him and ran back into the room. He didn't stop until he was standing right in front of the king. "I know I'm not supposed to be here," he said, his voice quivering, "but I have important news. We discovered a lava flow just outside the village. We think the volcano's ready to erupt. You need to do something!"

"Who is this child?" bellowed the king.

"Nobody important. He's leaving," said the chief. "Now!"

Josh took a step toward the king. "There's lava outside. It's red-hot and moving down the path." He grabbed the king by the arm. "You've got to come see it."

The room fell silent. One of the king's bodyguards gasped. Josh looked around, confused, and then quickly released the king's arm.

"You have broken the kapu. Nobody touches the king, especially not a commoner and a foreigner like you," thundered the chief. He tried to grab Josh, but Josh darted out of the way. He ran through the door, out to his siblings and Pilikia.

"Follow me! Run!" yelled Josh as he whizzed by. The three of them watched, stunned, as he tore through the crowd that had assembled to see the king. The chief and the priest's assistants streamed out of the temple after him. "There he is," shouted the chief. "Stop him!"

The crowd parted, allowing the priest's assistants to run through. Six of the king's bodyguards emerged from the temple and raced with them down the path after Josh.

"Where is he going? What should we do?" cried Will.

Ellen watched as more people streamed down the path. "We need to catch up with him."

"He might be going to the City of Refuge," said Pilikia.

"What's that?" asked Will.

"It's a place where people go if they are in trouble. I don't know what Josh did, but judging by all the people chasing him, I'd say it was bad. If he makes it there alive, the priest in the City of Refuge will perform a special ceremony so he'll be forgiven. Then he can return to the village safely."

"That makes sense," said Ellen. "Can you take us there?"

Pilikia nodded.

"Then what are we waiting for? Let's go."

— TEN —

JOSH'S NEW FRIEND

When Josh reached the break in the path, he stopped, unsure which way he should turn. *Everyone will be expecting me to go to the City of Refuge, so that's the last place I should go. Maybe I should leave the path altogether. That would really confuse them.*

He ran part way down the path to the City of Refuge before veering off into the underbrush. Every time he heard a noise he ducked behind some of the tall ferns and waited until the coast was clear.

It was hard work hiking through the rainforest. Without a path to guide him, Josh had no idea where he was going. Occasionally, he saw a sliver of sky between the trees. His calves began to ache, making him aware that he was slowly moving uphill. The ferns became thinner and the clumps of moss that lined the forest floor sparser. Josh found himself picking up speed even though his legs burned.

Before long he was halfway between the village and the top of the mountain. The peak above him was almost barren; only a few trees dotted its sides. Josh stood still for a moment. As he took in his lonely surroundings, all he could hear was the wind. He couldn't see another soul. He swallowed as he blinked rapidly, trying to hold back his tears.

The volcano loomed before him. "You don't look like a volcano. I don't know why we've been so worried about you," said Josh, staring at the summit. "Shouldn't you at least be cone shaped or have some smoke coming out of you or something?" The squawking of a bird was his only reply. "Maybe we were wrong about the lava. Maybe you're not an active volcano after all."

As he tried to decide what to do next, he spotted a rectangular building nestled in a scraggly clump of trees on the side of the volcano, almost hidden by an outcropping of rock. It appeared to be made of stone and timber, much like the temple in the village.

Josh rubbed his chin. "That's not far from here. I bet it would be a good place to spend the night." He picked a stick off the ground and twirled it around. "Okay," he said, sounding more determined than he actually felt. "Here I go."

The journey up the mountain was grueling, but Josh actually enjoyed it. He had to climb carefully to avoid tripping over the dried vines and small boulders that littered the ground, but it kept his mind off his situation. The farther he went, the steeper the climb became. The last few yards were sheer rock, but the climbing technique he had learned from Hawk on their last time-travel adventure allowed him to scale the rocks with confidence. He tucked his walking stick into the back of his shorts and pulled himself up one handhold at a time.

Josh was breathing heavily when he reached the building near the summit. He pulled himself over the rocky ledge and rolled across the ground, panting. As he lay there, his legs slowly lost their jellylike feeling and his breathing gradually returned to normal.

The building was set on a platform of rocks. Its roof was made of dry rushes, just like the roofs in Pilikia's village, but nobody seemed to be maintaining it—it was full of huge, gaping holes. The walls were lined with columns of twigs that had been strung together into long sheets, but they, too, had chunks missing. The timbers that formed the building's frame were the only part of the building that looked strong.

Josh climbed onto the terrace that surrounded the building. There was no railing or other barrier to separate it from its surroundings. When he reached the front of the building, he leaned over and peered down the mountain. Everything began to go fuzzy. He shuffled backward until his heels connected with the wall behind him, and then he spread his hands out, his palms flat against the sheets of twigs. "That feels better," he murmured to himself. "It's a long way down." The breeze picked up and dropped a leaf near his feet. "Maybe I should go inside. It's getting windy out here."

He finished his circuit of the building, taking care to stay as far from the edge of the terrace as possible, and walked through the doorway. The inside of the building reminded him of the temple in Pilikia's village. A wooden statue with a red cloth tied around its neck dominated one corner. Piles of wrapped bundles littered the floor. Josh walked over and picked one up. Someone had carefully overlapped a series of leaves and folded them in half to form a bag. The bag was tied shut with a garland of twigs and berries. Judging from the smell wafting out of it, something was wrapped in the bag, probably food. Josh was still fingering the bundle when he heard a voice echo through the room.

"What are you doing?"

He spun around. A thin, middle-aged man stood in the doorway. He wore a loose-fitting tunic made of brown material. A tattered cape was flung haphazardly over one of his shoulders. He ran his hand through his matted hair as he studied his uninvited guest.

"Oh ... I ... um ... I was just out for a hike and thought it would be fun to look around. This building's pretty nice," stammered Josh.

"You can tell me the truth. I won't hurt you," said the man.

"Okay, well, this building seems to be falling apart."

"I know." The man looked at Josh carefully. "How did you get here?"

Josh's cheeks burned. "Well, it's kind of a long story, but I time traveled here, and then I got into a lot of trouble with the priest and the chief and then the king, who was visiting the village, so I climbed up here. I'm hoping everyone will think I went to the City of Refuge because I don't want them to find me." He closed his eyes and took a deep breath. It felt good to tell the truth.

Josh looked back at the man. His eyes were gentle. For reasons he didn't understand, Josh felt safe. "What's your name?" he asked.

"Pili Lani."

Josh scrunched up his nose. "Pee-lee lah-nee? Why do you guys always pick names with the word 'pee' in them?"

"It means 'close to heaven.' My grandmother chose it for me. She knew in her heart that I'd be a priest one day."

Josh felt his body deflate. "You're a priest?"

"Is that a problem?"

"Only if I do the wrong thing, which I probably will, because then I'll get into trouble with you, too."

"I'll make you a deal. If you do something wrong, I'll tell you. I won't punish you the first time, but if you deliberately do it again...." He gave Josh a lopsided smile. "Well, I probably wouldn't do anything then, either, because I'm really glad you're here. It gets lonely up here sometimes. I could use a friend."

Josh smiled back. "That's the best thing I've heard all day. By the way, I'm Josh. Would you mind if I called you P. L. for short?"

"That's fine with me. Are you hungry?"

"I'm always hungry."

"Then come out back. I do all my cooking outside. You can help me prepare our meal."

After a hearty meal of chicken and breadfruit, Josh and P. L. sat on the edge of the terrace in front of the temple and watched the sunset. It was the most beautiful thing Josh had ever seen; the view from the summit was outstanding. The mountain directly below them was barren and desolate, but farther away it became greener and lusher. Josh could see the ocean a long way past the village.

A dark gray haze hung over the land nearest the water, so Josh knew it must be raining there. He could see the magnificent colors of a rainbow. They reminded him of the promise of the rainbow in the Bible, that God would never send another flood to destroy the earth. *Maybe it's a promise to me, too. I hope you're with me, God. Maybe that's why I found P. L. Maybe you do answer prayer.*

He looked over to his new friend. "Can I ask you a question?"

P. L. nodded.

"Do you think the volcano's dangerous? My brother thinks it's going to erupt any minute, but Pilikia, my friend from the village, keeps telling us everything's okay. What do you think?"

P. L. pondered Josh's question. "I think Pele is preparing a surprise. My people think we're safe because there hasn't been an eruption for many generations, but I've heard strange rumblings in the earth and seen things never seen before. They may be a warning of things to come."

"What sort of things?"

"Like puddles of boiling water, bad smells, small lava flows, even a mild earthquake. Pele is unhappy. That's why I came up here to leave her offerings. There's just one problem: They're not working."

"If you think the volcano's going to erupt any minute, why are you still here? Shouldn't you go back to the village and warn everyone?"

"I didn't say she was going to erupt 'any minute.' I said I think she's preparing a surprise for us. It could be seasons before we experience anything more. Life unfolds slowly on the island."

"How will you know when it's time to go?"

"I don't know. It's been so long since we've had an eruption."

"You don't have a plan?"

P. L. let out a long sigh. "It's not that simple. First of all, it's not up to me to make a plan. That's the chief's job, and so far he doesn't think we need one."

"If you did make a plan, what would it be?"

P. L. chuckled. "You're not going to give up, are you?"

"Nope. I want to know what to do if the volcano erupts." As Josh waited for P. L.'s reply, he crossed and uncrossed his legs, wiggled his fingers, and rubbed the back of his neck, all the while looking extremely uncomfortable.

"Josh, I don't have a plan, but if you like, I can make one up for you. I'd be happy to do that if it would make you feel better."

Josh was quiet for a moment. "Can I tell you a secret?" he whispered.

P. L. nodded.

"Remember how I said my brother and sister and I get to time travel? We've been to a lot of different places, and every place we've visited had a problem that we helped fix. We think that's why we go on these journeys, you know, to help people. I don't know why we were sent here, but I feel like it has something to do with the volcano and me. That's why I need to know what to do if the volcano erupts. Where should I go? Is there a safe place to hide?" His voice grew higher and his words spilled out faster. "I saw a movie once about a volcano; the lava was really bad. You didn't want to be anywhere near it; it burned everything it touched. What should I do if I see some lava? What if I can't get out of the way?"

"You know, Josh, you're right. This mountain, Pele's home, is not something to take lightly. If Pele decides to erupt, there's not a lot you can do. Stay away from the lava, and most important of all, get as far away from the volcano as you can."

"That's the plan?" said Josh.

"Yes, that's the plan. Get out of the way as fast as you can. It's pretty simple."

"But what exactly does 'get out of the way' mean? Am I supposed to run to the other side of the island? Should I try to get to the ocean? I want to know exactly what to do."

P. L. sighed. "I can't tell you exactly what to do because it depends on how the eruption unfolds. In the past, parts of the island have usually been spared, so we traveled to those parts, but my ancestors experienced eruptions that were so ferocious there was no safety to be found anywhere."

"What about the water?" asked Josh.

"When Pele is thinking about erupting, she often sends an earthquake as a warning. This stirs up the ocean, creating enormous waves. At times like this, being in the water is even more dangerous than being on land."

"Great," muttered Josh, "just great. The only place left to go is the air." He sat there for a minute, pressing the palm of his hand against his forehead. "Think, think, think." Suddenly a huge smile crossed his face. His eyes sparkled with newfound hope. "Maybe that would work. Maybe we could fly out of this place."

P. L. looked at him, confused. "Fly? Only birds do that."

"Actually, where I come from, people can … oh, never mind. It's too hard to explain. You wouldn't happen to have a hang glider, would you?"

P. L. looked even more confused.

Josh let out a deep breath. "I guess not. There's got to be something we can do. I need a plan."

"I have a suggestion," said P. L. "If the volcano erupts and there's no earthquake, it may be possible to travel to one of the neighboring islands by canoe. Do you know where we keep the canoes?"

Josh shook his head.

P. L. stood up and pointed to a break in the trees along the coastline. "See that clearing?"

Josh nodded.

"That's where the canoes are stored. If you take the lava tube the journey is actually quite easy."

Josh frowned. "Are you sure about that?"

"It's perfectly safe to travel down that particular lava tube. It's been empty for a long, long time."

"What do I do if I get to the canoes?"

"Follow the others. My people have been navigating the seas for generations."

"How can you navigate without a compass?"

P. L. gave him another confused look. "A what?"

Josh took the compass from around his neck and handed it to P. L. His friend examined it from every angle, entranced.

"I've never seen anything like this. Where did you get it?"

"It was a gift from my grandparents."

"What does it do?"

"It tells me what direction I'm going. I have no idea how you can navigate the ocean without one. They come in handy, you know."

"I was a navigator before I became a priest. My people have many ways to guide us as we travel." P. L. handed the compass back to Josh. "Ways that don't include your little tool."

Josh hung the compass back around his neck. "Like what?"

"We memorize every detail about the route we are traveling—every little thing that might impact our journey is mentally noted and reviewed. That way we can easily turn around at any time and find our way home. You can always tell which person in the canoe is the navigator; he's the one with the bloodshot eyes. It's a big responsibility keeping track of all those details—navigators don't get much sleep.

"Once we've aligned our canoe with the landmarks, we look to the sky to confirm our orientation. The rising and setting of certain stars help guide us."

"What if there are lots of clouds and you can't see the stars?"

"That's a good question. The ocean swells guide us too. The familiar wave patterns give us a sense of direction."

"But I've watched waves before. It seems like they're always changing."

"It may seem like that, but they have predictable patterns we've memorized over time. The daily flights of certain birds also help us.

Some of them travel great distances for fish every day. It's amazing what you can learn when you stop and observe life around you."

"Oh, brother," muttered Josh. "What is it with you jungle people? Some of the other people we visited said stuff like that too. I like to get up and get going. I don't spend a lot of time thinking about what's happening around me. I just do my own thing and forget about watching everything else."

"I understand why you might want to do that, but then you're—"

A deep rumble erupted from inside the earth. The mountain began to shake. Josh and P. L. looked at each other. It took P. L. a few seconds to react. He grabbed Josh, dragged him into the building, and crouched over top of him as they waited for the trembling to stop. Josh couldn't see much—P. L.'s body was blocking most of his view—but out of the corner of his eye he could see the twig walls shaking.

The trembling stopped as quickly as it had begun. Before P. L. could sit up, another tremor hit. P. L. landed on top of Josh seconds before the roof collapsed. Pieces of it landed on the floor on either side of them.

Josh struggled to breathe under P. L.'s weight. His legs and arms started to go numb, but he didn't dare move. As he waited for the shaking to stop he could hear the walls crack. The floor continued to heave up and down. Even though the aftershock lasted only a few seconds, it seemed like hours.

Once the shaking stopped, P. L. scrambled to his feet and helped Josh up. They stood together surveying the damage. The temple was in ruins. The front wall that faced the ocean was gone; it had fallen down the side of the mountain. The thick timbers that supported the ceiling had snapped in half and were lying on the floor. The back wall was partially intact, but huge holes had been ripped in the twig walls. A crevice ran down the center of the floor. Hot, smelly wisps of steam drifted out of it.

Josh looked up at P. L. "That wasn't good, was it?"

"You can say that again. We'd better go warn the villagers, but I need to leave an offering for Pele first."

"But you said your offerings weren't working. What's the point?"

"It can't hurt. I'll just be a minute and then we'll be off."

ELEVEN

TERROR

❂▣❂▣❂▣❂▣❂▣❂▣❂

can't go back to the village, remember?" said Josh. "If the chief sees me, I'll be in big trouble."

"But we can't stay here. It's not safe on the mountain," said P. L.

"What about the City of Refuge? Maybe I should go there."

P. L. furrowed his brow. "The chief might have men waiting for you outside the city gates. You'd never make it past them." He paused for a minute as he considered Josh's situation, and then he put his hands on Josh's shoulders and looked him square in the eye. "You're coming with me. I'll talk to the chief. In light of our circumstances," he continued, sweeping his arms back to take in the destruction around them, "I'm sure he'll let you in."

Josh's stomach ached at the thought of returning to the village, but he was relieved to get off the mountain. He followed P. L. through the misshapen doorway on the back wall, stepping carefully to avoid the fallen debris. A loud roar erupted from the summit, catching them both off guard. Josh looked up and gasped. The summit was glowing from what appeared to be an incredible display of yellow and orange fireworks. Molten lava spewed up in a fountain high into the air, illuminating the dark sky with ribbons of light. The spray faded to black as it cascaded onto the barren rock below.

Josh reluctantly looked away from the fireworks and put his hand on P. L.'s arm. "Have you ever seen anything like that before?"

"We haven't had a show like this for many generations," said P. L., not taking his eyes off the summit. "We'd better hurry."

The two of them stumbled down the mountain in the twilight. They were halfway to the village before Josh looked back. The lava fountain had already begun to fade. When Josh glanced back a minute later it had fizzled to nothing.

"Look, P. L., it's gone. Where did it go?" he asked.

"I don't know," said P. L., using the side of a large boulder to help himself balance. "We'll worry about that later. We need to get to the village." He picked up the pace, practically sliding down a steep slope of pebbles in his hurry to return to his people.

The closer they got to the village, the faster Josh's heart began to pound. He began to pray. *God, this isn't good. That volcano is doing strange things, and I'm going back to a village where everyone hates me. I don't know why I'm even talking to you about this because I don't think you can hear me, but somehow it seems like the right thing to do. Please don't let the chief hurt me or let the lava get us. It would be really good if you could send us the time stone right now. We need to get out of here before things get even worse.*

"It's a good thing Ellen didn't hear that prayer," he muttered to himself. "She'd probably say it's wrong to pray like that, but I don't care. I think it's better to tell God what you're really thinking than to not say anything at all."

P. L. stopped when they reached the edge of the village. "Whatever you do, keep quiet. I'll do the talking. The chief will listen to me once I tell him about Pele's eruption. The less he hears from you, the better."

"But what if I have something important to say?"

"Save it for later," ordered P. L.

P. L. strode confidently into the village, walking past the huts of sleeping villagers. Josh had to hustle to keep up with him. He looked for Will and Ellen; there was no sign of them anywhere. When they reached the chief's hut, P. L. marched up to the doorway, grabbed the sleeping guard by the shoulder, and gave him a firm shake. "I need to speak with the chief," he ordered. "Get him, now!"

The guard blinked rapidly. It took him a few seconds to clear his head. "What's your business? The chief doesn't like to be disturbed in the middle of the night."

P. L. glared at him. "Get him now, or I'll tell him his night watchman was sleeping on the job."

The guard reluctantly got up and entered the hut. He emerged a minute later with the chief in tow. The chief's face grew stern when he spotted Josh, but P. L. gave him a curt nod and began to speak before he had time to comment on Josh's presence.

"Pele is unhappy. Our offerings have not satisfied her. She sent us a series of earthquakes and a lava fountain on the summit."

The chief looked toward the summit. Only a thin wisp of gray smoke was visible in the moonlight. There was no sign that anything out of the ordinary had just occurred.

The chief's eyes narrowed. "You woke me up for this?"

"It was going crazy before, honest," blurted out Josh. "We saw lava shooting into the air. I've never seen anything like it before. He's telling the truth."

The chief yawned. "Have there been any other signs?"

"I've seen smoke, a light sprinkling of ash, and felt small tremors the past few days," said P. L.

"Really? How come I didn't notice any of that stuff?" asked Josh.

"You were too busy getting into trouble," replied the chief.

"Oh." Josh looked away, his cheeks burning.

The chief turned to P. L. "None of those signs is out of the ordinary for our people. We experience them all the time."

There was a long silence. Finally, P. L. spoke. "There have been other signs too. Josh saw some lava, and even though there's no sign of it now I swear we just experienced an earthquake and a lava fountain. Pele is very unhappy. We need to do something. We can't wait any longer."

The chief deliberated for a minute. A determined look came over his face. He straightened up, pulling his shoulders back. "We need a better offering. We need to make Pele happy."

"It's too late. The signs we experienced today haven't been seen in many generations. We have to leave," insisted P. L. "Pele is very angry."

The chief glanced at Josh again. "The boy has caused trouble ever since he arrived. Maybe he is the source of Pele's anger. If we leave him as an offering, he may calm Pele's wrath."

The blood drained from Josh's face. "I know I was bad, but I wasn't that bad," he stammered. "This has nothing to do with me, honest. Volcanoes are a part of nature—you know, something the earth does every once in a while. It doesn't have anything to do with angry gods. Sacrificing me won't change anything. Your people need to get out of here before it's too late."

"What do you know about our gods? You came here uninvited, caused trouble, and now you're trying to tell me how to run my village?" demanded the chief.

P. L. shot Josh a warning look, but Josh was too busy staring at Pilikia to notice. He had just spotted her standing in a patch of woods behind the chief's hut, watching as he talked with P. L. and the chief. Josh gave her his saddest face in the hope that she would come over and help, but she pretended not to see him. He glanced back at P. L. When his gaze returned to the woods, Pilikia was gone.

I thought you were my friend—you were better than a sister. Families are supposed to stick together, no matter what. A tear rolled down his cheek and splashed onto his foot. *You should come back and help me. I know Ellen would do that for me.*

He couldn't stop his tears as he listened to P. L. and the chief arguing. They fiercely disagreed on what should be done. Josh took a step toward the woods where Pilikia had disappeared. It seemed like no one was looking so he took another and then another. He was almost at the tree Pilikia had been hiding behind, when the guard spotted him and dragged him back to the chief.

The chief stopped quarreling. "What's going on?" he demanded.

The guard thrust Josh toward him. Josh had to dig his feet into the dirt so he wouldn't crash into the chief. He knew if he touched him he'd upset the chief again and get into even more trouble.

"I caught the boy trying to escape," spat the guard.

The chief stared intently at Josh. "The boy will make a fine sacrifice. Someone who makes this much trouble will certainly satisfy Pele."

"No, not me! You've got the wrong guy!" Josh tried to get away. The guard grabbed him by the arm. "Ellen! Will! Pilikia! Help!" he screamed.

Josh's shouts woke up everyone in the village. They rushed out of their huts to see what was happening.

Josh looked through the crowd, trying to catch a glimpse of his brother and sister. Suddenly, he spotted them near the back. "Will, Ellen, help! They're going to kill me! Help! Save me!"

Josh's cry was answered by a faint trembling. It started slowly and was so subtle that anyone who didn't notice the air quivering would have missed it. The birds nesting in the trees woke up and began screeching as they took to the air.

The villagers fell silent and stared up at the sky in amazement. The trembling increased. The penned-up animals began bawling, running back and forth along their fences as they tried to escape. The ones that were free ran into the rainforest to hide.

The guard had let go of Josh, but the boy didn't dare move. He glanced down at the compass dangling from his neck and gawked at it, spellbound. The needle was spinning wildly even though Josh was facing north.

The vibrations continued to increase. Josh looked down, expecting to see the ground swelling beneath his feet, but it didn't look any different. It seemed like the vibrations should have been coming from deep within the earth, but they weren't—Josh could feel them in the air.

In the midst of all the confusion, Will and Ellen broke through the crowd and ran over to Josh. Ellen grabbed him by the arm. "What's going on?"

"I don't know. My friend P. L. thinks something's happening with the volcano. We saw some lava shooting out of it. The chief wants to sacrifice me so the eruption will stop."

"They think that would actually help?" asked Will.

Josh nodded. "We need to get out of here."

Ellen turned and looked around. They were surrounded by people. "How?"

"I don't know. If you get a chance, make a run for it."

"Shouldn't we stick together? I don't want to go into the jungle by myself."

Josh looked out over the crowd. "Do you remember that clearing we were in before?"

"Which one?" asked Ellen.

Just then an enormous explosion shook the mountain. A massive cloud of white smoke billowed out of its peak. Two more ground-shaking explosions followed. Huge boulders shot from the summit and rolled down the mountain. A massive surge of red-hot lava poured down the mountain, completely enveloping everything in its path.

Panic erupted throughout the crowd as the villagers realized the lava was flowing in their direction. Family members quickly banded together and fled. Ellen grabbed Josh and Will by the arms. "Let's get out of here, now!"

— TWELVE —

EXPLOSION

They had only run a few steps down one of the paths when they came upon a group ahead of them. A family of six—a mom and dad, three young children, and an elderly grandmother—blocked their way. The grandmother was so thin and weak that she could barely walk. The children screamed with each new belch of the earth beneath them.

Ellen rushed ahead and went alongside the grandmother, holding her arm to steady her. The old woman nodded gratefully but kept her focus on the path ahead as she struggled to keep up with her family.

Josh looked around, frustrated that Ellen and the grandmother were slowing him down. He sped up, closing the gap between him and the family, and tried to nudge his way past Ellen and the grandmother. Ellen moved over, giving him room to grab the grandmother's other arm so he could help her along too. He shook his head and pointed straight ahead. When Ellen realized that he wanted to run past them, she shot him a dirty look and moved to the middle of the path, blocking him and anyone else who might want to pass.

Josh looked behind him, getting more frustrated by the minute. Will was jogging along, constantly turning back to see if the lava was catching up with them. Josh slowed his pace slightly. As he took a deep breath, he noticed the air was getting warmer.

113

Just then Will caught up with him. "We've got to get out of here," he panted, wiping the sweat off his forehead. "The lava will be here any minute."

Josh looked back. The lava was coming down the path after them, only minutes away, enveloping the trees and shrubs in flames. When he glanced up at the summit, he realized that a second lava stream had started. As the two streams ran down the mountain they moved closer together, combining into one powerful, gushing flow.

"Oh, no," cried Josh. "Hurry! Let's get Ellen."

With just a few steps the boys caught up to their sister. Josh grabbed Ellen's left arm and Will grabbed her right. Before she even realized what was happening, they had pulled her away from the grandmother who by now was completely exhausted.

Ellen tried to get away from her brothers, but they wouldn't let go of her. "Leave me alone! I need to help her!"

"The lava's almost here. We need to hurry," shouted Will.

They were about twenty steps ahead of the family, almost at the edge of the rainforest, when Ellen dug in her heels. The three of them skidded to a stop. Ellen broke away from the boys and spun around, ready to go back to the grandmother. Before she could move, a horrible cracking noise reverberated through the forest.

She turned forward again and followed Josh. He led her and Will to a flat patch of swirly black rock up ahead. They ran across it and joined a group of villagers who were staring at a huge hole in the ground. The rock had caved in, revealing a wide, fast-flowing river of lava traveling right beneath their feet.

Waves of heat poured out of the hole. Will backed up. His eyes began to roll. Ellen guided him away from the lava before he had a chance to faint.

Josh slowly crept closer to the opening, mesmerized by the orange swirls of molten rock coursing down the lava tube. The heat was oppressive. He could barely breathe and his feet couldn't stand the heat. He lifted them up and down in a crazy dance just to stay in place. Suddenly, he realized his ears were hot; they felt like they were on fire. He placed his palms on top of them to protect them, his gaze never leaving the opening. Sweat poured out of every pore in his body. The sound of Ellen's voice broke through his trance. He turned and ran back across the clearing to his siblings.

The three kids huddled together, watching the villagers pour out of the rainforest. The family they had followed limped along. The children and grandmother were already worn out. They headed to the other side of the clearing where the path continued on to the ocean.

Josh turned back to the mountain. The original lava flow had slowed down and was now inching instead of rushing down the mountain, but the summit was ablaze from an even bigger lava fountain that shrouded the mountain in a yellow-orange glow. Lava continued to pour out of new openings on the summit's sides, creating a steady river that had almost reached Pilikia's village.

"The lava is going to destroy everything. Can't anyone do something to stop it?" asked Josh.

"Like what?" said Will. "You're talking about tons of molten rock."

"I suppose. I just feel so helpless."

They watched in horror as the lava hit the village. The trees on either side of it went up in flames. Within minutes, the lava set fire to the temple. Its twig walls and straw roof ignited like a row of matches, causing it to collapse into a fiery heap. The burning temple had a domino-like effect on the rest of the village. The straw huts caught fire one after another until the entire village was aflame.

Josh turned away from the spectacle so he could check the lava tube. Even though he wasn't right next to it, he could tell the level of the lava was rising. It was still flowing beneath the top layer of rock, but fist-sized balls of lava were splashing out of the hole, coating the rock around the opening with sparkly orange splatter.

The last group of villagers ran through the clearing carrying baskets of clothing and cooking supplies. One of the women stopped for a moment. "Get out of here," she ordered.

"But the lava on the summit is slowing down," said Josh.

"It could speed up. Go!"

"She's right. Let's get out of here," urged Will.

Josh, Will, and Ellen quickly fell in line behind the group of villagers. As they ran, a nervous feeling settled into Josh's stomach. He swallowed, trying to reassure himself that everything was okay. All of a sudden the hair on the back of his neck stood up. A split second later, a loud roar erupted from the lava tube. He turned around just in time to see a dome of lava break out above the opening he'd been standing by just a minute before. It shook as it floated in the air. Thin strands of lava broke off and sprayed in every direction.

Josh stared wide-eyed, not sure what to make of this strange phenomenon. Suddenly, the lava bubble collapsed inward, rejoining the molten lava flowing through the tunnel. An enormous trembling shook the ground. The lava river welled up again and poured out of the top of the opening, flowing toward the group like waves of red-hot water. It was brilliant red when it left the earth, but as it came in contact with the air, the middle of the stream hardened slightly, forming a silvery-gray film that floated on top of the molten lava. The air filled with smoke as the lava gushed, covering everything in its path.

The women and children began to scream. The men dropped the bundles they had been carrying and drove their families back onto the path, clutching their children in their arms as they fled. Josh, Will, and Ellen ran through the rainforest after them. It didn't take them long to catch up to the rest of the villagers. Josh spotted P. L. a few steps ahead, carrying an elderly man across his back. There was no sign of Pilikia or her family anywhere. He watched as a young man steered a mother and her baby through the crowd, toward the front of the line. He caught Will's eye. "Let's follow them."

Will nodded. He was so breathless he couldn't speak.

They snaked their way through the crowd, Josh first, followed by Will and then Ellen. It was hard for Josh to keep the young family within his sight, but with some tricky maneuvering he managed to lead his brother and sister along.

Josh had just passed P. L.—he was in the middle of the throng, still running with the elderly man on his back—when he lost track of the young man and the mother they'd been following.

Josh glanced back at Will, unsure of how to proceed, but Will had a glazed look in his eyes. He didn't seem to know what was going on. Josh spotted P. L. again, but he was focused on getting the elderly man and himself to safety. Ellen was too far behind to be of any help.

Another enormous belch sprang from the summit. A huge cloud of ash poured out and quickly traveled downwind to the villagers, coating them in an abrasive gray layer of volcanic dust. Josh tried to rub the ash off his arms and chest, scratching himself in the process, but it wouldn't come off. He was left with swirls of gray all over his body.

A massive roar followed the belch. Lava shot out of the summit in another fountain. This one seemed to reach the clouds. More lava gushed out of two new holes on the volcano's sides and rushed down the underground lava tubes. Everyone stopped moving—the ground was shaking so violently that it was impossible to walk. Josh grabbed onto Will and hung on tight. The sound of the earth heaving grew and grew until it was as loud as the roar of a jet at take-off. Josh let go of Will and covered his ears. He couldn't bear to listen to it any longer.

Suddenly, the shaking stopped. P. L. shifted the old man onto his back again and took a cautious step forward. He motioned to Josh with his head, inviting him to follow them. Josh didn't move. "Josh, hurry," he begged. "We don't have long. It's going to get worse."

The crowd surged ahead, forcing the kids along with them. Josh looked at P. L. "I'm going another way."

"What?"

"The group is too slow. I'm going on my own."

"No, Josh, you stay with ..."

Josh grabbed Will by the arm and led him off the path, into the rainforest.

"Where are we going?" gasped Will. "We can't leave the group. We're going to die!"

"We're taking a shortcut. Trust me," said Josh.

"Where's Ellen?"

Josh looked over his shoulder. "I don't know. We'll find her later."

"But ..."

Josh ignored Will's objections and continued cutting a path through the rainforest. It was hard, slow work. Five minutes later they had only traveled about a hundred meters.

Thick clouds of smoke drifted through the trees, but light still managed to penetrate the treetops. Everything was covered in ash, giving the area an unearthly appearance. The foliage became more and more dense. It seemed like the rainforest was closing in on them.

Will came to an abrupt stop. He put his hands on his hips and stared at his brother. "Where are you taking us?" he demanded.

"This is a shortcut. It'll be faster in the long run because we don't have all those old people and babies to slow us down."

"Have you ever been here before?"

"No," admitted Josh.

Will let out a deep breath. "So, you don't know where you're going?"

"Of course I know. We're going the same direction as the path, see?" He looked down at his compass, but the needle was still spinning around in circles.

"Great, now we're really in trouble. Your compass isn't even working. It doesn't matter; I can tell we're going the opposite direction of everyone else. We're going up, toward the volcano. That's why my calves hurt—we're traveling up, not down."

"Oh," said Josh in a small voice.

"We'll settle this later. Right now we need to get back on the path and join the others. I'm not wandering around the rainforest with you one second longer."

Josh watched as Will jogged back down the path they had just made. It wasn't hard for him to retrace his steps—their footprints had left a clear trail in the ash.

Josh rubbed his eyes, smearing ash into them. They began to burn. Tears poured down his cheeks, leaving pink streaks on his otherwise gray face.

His tears of fear and pain turned into tears of shame as he thought about how badly he'd behaved over the last few days. *Why can't I be good like everyone else? Will and Ellen never have problems like I do. It's so hard. I don't want to get into trouble, but I don't want to be like everyone else, either. I want to do my own thing.*

A crackling noise interrupted his thoughts. He turned to his left, upwind, and spotted a slow moving lava flow tumbling through the forest. The front edge of the lava glowed bright red. The back of the flow was covered in a thick, black crust.

As it moved along, the lava engulfed the base of some ohia trees, sending flames up their trunks and acrid smoke into the air. Soon entire trees, leaves and all, were ablaze. Small patches of brush caught fire as the lava came into contact with the wild grass and low-growing bushes.

Josh ran after Will. He had to stop every few seconds to catch his breath; it seemed like the smoke was sucking the air right out of his lungs. When he reached the end of the path, he made a sharp right onto the now-empty main path and stopped dead in his tracks.

A wide swath of lava was running across the path ahead of him. It had joined up with a lava stream from the other side, forming one immense river. There was no way Josh could move forward or to either side.

He turned and looked back up the mountain. Fresh lava was

flowing out of the new holes on its sides, feeding the streams that trapped him. The summit was still spewing steam and red-hot splatter in every direction.

Josh spun around and around, trying to find a way out. There was nowhere to go. His lower lip started to quiver. Fresh tears spilled out of his eyes.

"Oh, no," he wailed, "I'm trapped! What am I supposed to do?"

— THIRTEEN —

TRAPPED

A s Josh stared at the devastation around him, fire broke out on the land directly above him. Flames spread from tree to tree sending a shower of sparks everywhere. Within minutes the trees were reduced to burning skeletons. The air grew hotter and hotter. Breathing became unbearable. Josh put his hands over his mouth and nose, but it didn't help.

The lava inched forward, its top and sides continually hardening to a silvery black. His little island of safety was rapidly shrinking. Panic raced through his body, yet at the same time he felt more alive than he'd ever felt in his life. In his mind he knew he would die any minute, yet somehow his heart couldn't accept it.

God, I know I've been really bad, but I'm not ready to die yet. I don't know what you can do—it seems hopeless—but please help me. I want to go back to Mom and Dad with Will and Ellen and be a family again. Please don't let me get buried underneath all this lava.

The lava moved closer. Josh put his hands up to his mouth and began yelling at the top of his lungs. "Will, Ellen, help! I'm trapped! Somebody, help me!" Smoke burned in his lungs. "Please, someone, anyone, help!" he sputtered.

He looked behind him. The lava was only a short distance away.

A tiny whisper of sound caught his attention. He turned to his right. There was nothing. He turned to his left. There, on the other side of the lava river, stood Will, Ellen, P. L., Pilikia and her family, and the village chief. Ellen yelled something, but Josh couldn't hear her over the roar of the lava and the crackling of the flames. He pointed to the ground around him.

Josh could see the chief talking to P. L. *Oh, no,* he thought, *they're probably planning to leave me here as an offering for Pele.*

"Please, God," he whispered, "please don't leave me here. Please help me to get over to Will and Ellen. I promise I'll never be bad again."

Josh watched P. L. pull something that looked like an ax from his waistband. *Maybe they're going to kill me. I don't want to die.*

Will, P. L., Pilikia's family, and the chief disappeared. Ellen kept waving madly. Pilikia pointed at the rainforest behind them and flapped her arms back and forth.

The lava behind Josh continued to creep forward. Now it was only five meters away.

P. L. and the chief reappeared, rolling a large boulder. "What on earth are they doing?" exclaimed Josh, though no one could hear him. Ellen and Pilikia ran over and helped them push the rock to the edge of the lava flow. The chief looked up at Josh and shouted something. Then he and P. L. ran back into the rainforest.

The lava continued to stream closer. Josh watched helplessly as Ellen and Pilikia's family started shaking a tall ohia tree. It toppled over and landed on the boulder P. L. and the chief had just rolled into place.

The tree hung there, creating a bridge over the lava flow. Its tip didn't quite make it all the way over the lava flow. Lava splatter hit its dry leaves, causing them to burst into flame like a match that had just been struck. Its branches began smoldering too, sending more smoke Josh's way. Will and Ellen waved madly, trying to get Josh to jump onto the tree so he could crawl along the trunk over the rushing lava.

"I can't reach it," he shouted as the branches began to burn. Their waving grew more frantic. Josh shook his head. "I can't make it."

P. L. stripped off his robe, threw it to the ground, and took a cautious step onto the tree bridge. He dropped to his knees and began crawling across it, slowly at first, then quickly as the heat started to pound him.

His bravery inspired Josh. Josh took a few steps back and ran at the tree. When he reached the edge of the lava he jumped, landing halfway on the trunk and halfway across some branches. His body began sliding to one side. He grabbed onto one of the thicker branches and hung on for dear life. The tree sagged under his weight, moving him precariously close to the fiery lava. Blobs of splatter shot up, setting his branch on fire. He could feel the skin on his hands and legs burn. He pulled himself up and crawled along the tree. P. L. backed up, calling out words of encouragement.

Sweat poured off of Josh's forehead, sliding down his face into his eyes, making it hard to see. He squinted as he felt his way along the tree bridge. Time seemed to move in slow motion. The closer he got to the group, the better he could hear their cheers. Finally, his right hand reached out and felt only air. There was nothing to grab onto. He fell forward. Strong arms grabbed him, pulling him off the tree.

Josh heard a mighty roar, and everything went black.

— FOURTEEN —

HOMEWARD BOUND

Josh slowly opened his eyes. He didn't dare move; he felt like every cell in his body was on fire. It seemed like he was back in the rainforest. He could see a stand of tall ohia trees gently swaying in the early morning light. Bits of ash fell off their leaves, floating to the ground like snow.

At the sound of someone approaching, Josh closed his eyes, not wanting to face whomever was coming. The last thing he remembered was crawling across the tree bridge that spanned the lava river, his arms and legs hurting more than they'd ever hurt before, even more than when he fell off his bike in the third grade and broke his arm.

A soft hand touched his forehead, smoothing back his hair. *Mom,* he thought. A feeling of peace settled over him. *I miss her. I hope we go home soon.* The hands moved down his body, spreading a scented cream over his arms, legs, and chest. The gentle touch felt so good that he didn't dare open his eyes for fear that the person looking after him would stop.

The sound of a man's voice interrupted Josh's dreaming. Someone gently propped him up to a sitting position. He reluctantly opened his eyes. Will and Ellen hovered over him, looking concerned. Pilikia's mother and grandmother crouched beside him, rubbing the cream from their hands onto some ohia leaves that had blown to the ground. The chief and P. L. stood at his feet, staring at him. He gave them a weak smile.

"Will he survive?" asked the chief.

The women nodded. "He will feel better by tonight and should be able to get up tomorrow," said Pilikia's grandmother.

"Thank you," croaked Josh, his lips parched. He cleared his throat, hoping it would help him speak more clearly, but it made him cough instead. His chest heaved as he tried to catch his breath. Pilikia's grandmother leaned over and gently rubbed his back.

"Thank you," he whispered. "Thank you for taking care of me."

The sound of sniffling caught Josh's attention. He looked over to Will. Tears were pouring down his face. Will took off his glasses and wiped his eyes with his handkerchief, but by the time he put his glasses back on, he was crying even harder. A loud sob escaped from his chest and he began shaking uncontrollably. Ellen wrapped her arms around him. "It's okay, it's okay," she murmured over and over again. "Josh is going to be all right. It's over."

She didn't let go until Will had calmed himself down. He wiped his face one last time. Just when Josh thought everything was all right, Will got down on his knees and leaned over, staring at Josh with his red-rimmed, bloodshot eyes.

"You're lucky they're taking care of you. If it were up to me, I'd have left you out there, surrounded by all that lava. It would have served you right," declared Will.

"Will!" Ellen swatted him on the arm. "That's the last thing he needs to hear right now. Be nice. He's been through a lot."

"Only because he's so dumb." Will's voice turned into a sob. He took one deep breath after another as he tried to compose himself so he could continue. "You don't take off on everyone in the middle of a volcanic eruption when you have no idea what you're doing. That was just plain stupid."

"I'm sure he didn't mean to do that," said Ellen, but she sounded uncertain.

P. L. caught her eye. "I asked him to stay with us. He chose not to listen."

A silence fell over the group.

"I thought he was lost," said Ellen quietly.

Will shook his head. "He thought he knew better than everyone else. He dragged me off the trail so we could pass everyone. I came back to the group as soon as I realized what he was doing."

The chief sighed. "You've been trouble since the moment you arrived." There was a long pause while he stared at Josh. Josh swallowed repeatedly and looked from one face to the next. The chief shook his head and let out another sigh. Suddenly, Pilikia started to giggle. Ellen and the women joined in. Soon, everyone was laughing.

As the laughter faded, Josh sat up a little straighter. "Why did you save me?"

"When you come to our village, you become part of our family, whether we like you or not. That's how it works with our people. You didn't deserve our help; you behaved badly. That is why we banished you from the village. You were inconsiderate toward others, but we still offered you help because when you are here, you are a part of us. That's why we saved you."

"But you didn't want to save me at first," murmured Josh. "You kept talking about sacrificing me."

"We were wrong to think like that. It wouldn't have made any difference."

"That's what I kept trying to tell you."

"If you had listened to P. L. in the first place," interrupted Will, "none of this would have happened."

The chief lowered his eyebrows and gave Will a stern look. Will blushed furiously and looked away.

"You would have been safe with my people farther down the mountain. We know the best places to hide when danger strikes—this knowledge has been with us for many generations. When you decided that you knew more than we did, you insulted us and the lessons we've learned over our lifetimes. Your actions were wrong. You need to learn to respect and obey your elders, not go your own way."

Josh's face felt hot. Tears pooled in eyes. He scrunched his eyes shut, trying to hold the tears in. It took a minute before he felt calm enough to speak.

"I'm sorry," he mumbled, looking at the chief's knees.

"Stand up," ordered the chief.

Josh tried to stand. As he struggled to his feet, he noticed that the skin on the front of his calves and on the palms of his hands was completely black. The black faded into raw red blisters along the sides of his legs and his arms. His skin flexed as he moved. The pain was so intense it paralyzed him. The women put their hands under his armpits and helped him up, holding onto him to keep him steady.

"Look into my eyes," said the chief.

Josh struggled to meet his gaze.

"Part of being a man is apologizing with honor."

Josh gulped. "I … I … I'm sorry." Shame filled his heart. For the first time since they arrived, he truly realized how badly he'd behaved. "I don't know why I thought I knew so much—I don't know anything. I should have listened, especially to you and P. L. I promise I'll behave better from now on. Can you forgive me?"

"Yes." The chief gave him a reassuring smile. "We accept your apology."

The rest of the day passed quickly. Josh had a long nap while Will, Ellen, and Pilikia circulated through the clearing, looking for anyone who might need help. The lava had stopped flowing and had hardened, leaving a wide patch of untouched rainforest for the people to rest in. Even the summit seemed calm. The occasional burst of smoke and the new volcanic rock were the only signs that something catastrophic had just occurred.

Will and Ellen picked up fallen branches, prepared food, entertained the children, and checked on Josh. Pilikia kept busy assisting her mother and grandmother as they looked after the villagers' medical needs, fetched water and other supplies, and helped change bandages. She passed by Josh several times during the day, but she didn't stop, which was quite fine with him. Josh was still upset that she hadn't helped him when he and P. L. were talking with the chief. After all they'd been through, it bothered him that she pretended not to see him.

As night approached, Will and Ellen settled in among a lush thicket of ferns next to Josh. Animals scurried and twittered around them, but the unfamiliar sounds didn't bother them anymore.

Ellen snuggled up to Josh. "Are you feeling better?" she asked.

"A lot better. I don't know what's in that cream they spread on my burns, but it sure works. We should bring some home."

Will sat up abruptly. "Why? Do you think you'll be crossing more lava rivers at home?"

"Of course not. I thought it might come in handy if we get a burn from the oven or something. Dad is always burning himself on the oven door." Josh glanced at his sister. "I guess that's who Will gets his lack of coordination from."

Ellen smiled. "When you start picking on Will, I know you're feeling better."

"I think you should go back to being sick," pouted Will.

"This is not the time to start a fight," said Ellen.

"Fine. We won't fight right now." There was a long pause. "Maybe later," added Will.

"You're impossible," groaned Ellen. She turned back to Josh. "You know, Josh, there's just one thing I don't understand. Why did you leave us when we were running from the lava? We're new here, and we'd never experienced a volcano before. Why did you think you knew better than everyone else?"

Josh tried to use his elbows to prop himself up, but it hurt too much to move. He had to settle for lying on his back, staring up at the stars in the night sky as he pondered her question. "I've been thinking about that since this morning. I didn't think I knew better than everyone else. It's more that I was impatient. Everybody was moving so slowly. I wanted to get away from the lava. I was tired of helping the old people and the mothers and babies. I thought that if we passed them, we could get to the end of the trail quicker."

"Why would you think that? You don't just ignore people who need help because you don't feel like slowing down. That doesn't make sense, and it sure doesn't match what the Bible says or anything Mom and Dad have taught us," scolded Ellen.

"But everything was so mixed up. That volcano was scary. I couldn't think straight."

"Ellen and I were in the exact same situation as you and we didn't do anything stupid like that," argued Will.

"Actually, you did something halfway stupid. You followed him," said Ellen.

"I know. I'll never do that again."

"Thanks," muttered Josh. He rolled over, turning his back to them, and fell into a restless sleep.

It was still dark when P. L. crept into the thicket and woke the three of them up. "Get up," he whispered, "I've got something to show you."

They stumbled to their feet, half asleep, and wandered out of the clearing after him.

"Where are you taking us?" asked Will.

"I discovered another lava flow. You have to see it."

The thought of seeing more lava woke everyone up in a hurry. "I'll stay back," said Will. "That way I'll be ready to go if something bad happens. Besides, I've seen enough lava to last me the rest of my life."

"Come on," said P. L., putting his arm around Will's shoulders. "There's nothing to be scared of. This one is safe, and it's not too far. You won't regret it."

As they ambled along, the rainforest gave way to the barren rock left thousands of years ago by previous volcanic eruptions. It was rough and jagged, the opposite of the smooth, swirly flows Josh had seen before. He hobbled a few steps behind everyone, not realizing the sharp edges of the rock were cutting his feet. The heat from the lava had permanently damaged the nerves on the soles of his feet.

A stiff breeze blew off the ocean, causing his hair to whip into his eyes. Ellen held back her ponytail as best she could.

As they approached the shoreline they could hear the pounding of the surf. Clouds of steam billowed up from the ocean, captivating Josh. If he used his imagination he could see all sorts of interesting shapes in the steam.

When he turned to speak to his brother he realized Will was trailing along farther behind him. "Hey, Will, what's taking you so long? Hurry up! I think we're almost there."

Will slowed down even more. "I'll stay back here and keep an eye on things."

Josh shrugged. "Okay. Do whatever you want. I hope you don't regret it."

The rest of the group moved forward. Eventually Will's curiosity got the better of him, and he rejoined P. L. and his siblings.

P. L. led them along the high cliffs that bordered the coastline, making sure they stayed well away from the edge. As they moved closer to the steam, the wind carried its tiny droplets toward them, drenching them in warm vapor.

P. L. climbed up a large outcropping of rock and pointed down the cliff. Josh heard the loud roaring of lava, but he couldn't see anything. The cloud of steam was too thick.

A sudden gust of wind blew the steam upward. Josh's jaw dropped when he spotted a red-hot lava flow shooting out of the side of the cliff, like water spraying out of a fire hose. It shot straight through the air before arcing into the ocean below. Great billows of steam rose from the spot where the lava hit the water.

Josh turned to P. L. "That's incredible! I've seen lava move slow, fast, shoot up in a fountain, and now this. That's one talented volcano."

P. L. smiled. "That's an interesting way of looking at it. I've never thought of volcanoes as talented, only powerful."

A movement behind a nearby rock caught Josh's eye. He watched as a slight bulge rose from the top of the rock. He grabbed P. L. by the arm and pointed. "There's something behind that rock. Did you see it?"

"I don't see anything," said P. L. "You're imagining things. You've been staring at the lava for too long."

"What if there's an animal back there?"

P. L.'s eyes scanned the rock and the area around it. "You're seeing things."

"No, I'm not. There's something behind that rock. Do you think you could go check?"

P. L. strode over to the rock and peered over it. A big smile crossed his face. Pilikia reluctantly stood up from her hiding place.

"Oh, it's her," said Josh. "I don't want to talk to her right now."

"I thought you two were best friends. You were sure in a hurry to ditch us for her the other day," said Ellen.

"Trust me, it was a big mistake. She totally ignored me when I really needed her. She's one of those people who only thinks about herself."

"Kind of like you," Ellen observed. Josh was too ashamed by the truth in her words to reply.

P. L. and Pilikia walked over to them. "Josh, I found your friend," said P. L.

"I'm not sure if she's still my friend," he pouted.

P. L. turned to Pilikia. "What's this all about?"

Pilikia shrugged her shoulders. "I don't know. Josh hasn't talked to me all day."

Josh glared at her. "Don't play dumb. You know exactly why I'm mad at you. You'd be mad at me if I treated you like that too."

"Pilikia?" said P. L.

She gave P. L. an embarrassed smile. "I think Josh is mad at me because I didn't help him when you and the chief were talking about sacrificing him to Pele. I was scared and didn't want to get into trouble. Besides, you and the chief wouldn't have listened to me anyway. Nobody cares about what I think."

"Now Pilikia, there's no need to feel sorry for yourself. If you didn't help your friend when he needed you, shouldn't you apologize to him?"

Pilikia stared at the ground between her feet.

"You pretended you didn't see me when I really needed you. I thought we were best friends; it seemed like you were practically my sister. That's not how you treat people, especially your family."

"I'm sorry," mumbled Pilikia. "I shouldn't have pretended I didn't know you; I should have helped you. You're right—we were best friends. I've had more fun with you than I've had with anyone in a long time." Her eyes filled with tears. "I'm sorry."

"It's okay. I made way more mistakes than you," said Josh quietly. "Nobody's perfect."

"Especially not you," added Will.

Ellen gave him a withering look.

Josh extended his hand toward Pilikia for their secret handshake. She put her hand on top of his fist, lightly so she didn't hurt him, and then he put down his other hand, followed by hers. "On the count of three," he said. "One. Two. Three." They lifted their arms into the air and shouted, "Friends."

"I'm glad you two made up, but it sounds like we need to have a talk," said P. L. He sat down on the rocks. Ellen, Pilikia, and Will plopped down beside him.

"Do you mind if I stand?" asked Josh. "It hurts too much to sit."

"No problem," said P. L. "I think everyone's learned an important lesson here."

"Is this going to be like those talks our dad gives us when we're in trouble?" asked Will.

Ellen glared at him. "Will, don't be rude. You're embarrassing me."

"I'd like to hear what you have to say, P. L.," said Josh.

P. L. smiled. "It's quite simple. There are lots of people who will be important to you during your lifetime, but some of the most important will be your family. Our families stay with us our entire lives. We're put into families because we need each other, so it's important that we treat our family members with respect, especially those who are older than us."

"I agree," said Josh. "I'm going to be much more respectful."

P. L. smiled. "Yes, Josh, I know you will. You've learned a lot these past few days."

"There's just one thing I don't understand."

"What's that?" asked P. L.

"This is our fifth time-travel mission. On each one of the other trips we helped the people we visited. I don't feel like we've done anything to help you."

"You're right. All you've done is made trouble for everyone," said Will.

"Thanks," muttered Josh. "I'm trying to be serious. If we weren't sent here to help your village, then why did we come?"

The five of them sat quietly, mulling over Josh's question.

"I don't know if this makes any sense, but I think we were sent here to learn something," said Ellen.

"I've been thinking the same thing," replied Josh. "I think it has to do with me and the volcano."

"You sure got us into a lot of trouble because you didn't listen," added Will.

"Thanks for reminding me. I'd forgotten."

"No problem," said Will, completely missing Josh's sarcasm.

"You know, P. L.," continued Josh, "I think it might have something to do with families. That's come up over and over again. The chief said that we became part of the family of your village when we came. You just talked about how families are with us our entire lives and we have to respect our elders. Maybe that's what we were supposed to learn."

"If you had listened to your elders in the first place, most of the bad stuff we went through wouldn't have happened," said Will.

Josh stuck out his tongue at Will and made a very rude face. "Would you stop blaming me for everything? I'm getting sick and tired of it."

"I'm only blaming you because you did so many things wrong."

"Guys," said Ellen, her voice raised, "that's enough. Will, leave him alone. He gets your point. And Josh, you need to listen better. I think that's been made perfectly clear."

"Great, now you're picking on me too," grumbled Josh.

"It's okay, Josh." P. L. spoke gently. "You came through in the end and made things right. In the long run, that's what matters. It's impossible to do things right all the time, but as long as we keep learning from our mistakes, we'll improve with time. You made some mistakes, you said you were sorry, we forgave you, and now you get a fresh start. See, everything's going to be just fine."

Josh wiped the tears from his eyes. "Thanks," he sniffled, rubbing his runny nose on the side of his arm. "I'm glad someone believes in me." As he leaned over to give P. L. a hug, the cord on his compass broke. The compass clattered across the rocks and settled in a narrow crevice. He shuffled over to it and reached down into the crack to pick it up. As his fingers touched the rock, a jolt of electricity ran up his arm. "Ouch!"

Ellen and Will ran over to his side. "What happened? Did something sting you?" asked Ellen.

"I don't know. When I reached down to grab my compass, I got a shock."

The three of them stared into the crevice. A big smile settled on Will's face and then Ellen's, and finally Josh's.

"I'm not ready to go home," said Josh.

Will shrugged. "You don't have much choice. It's time." He bent over and pulled the time stone out of the crevice. A whirlwind swirled across the cliffs, lifted the three of them up, and transported them home.

Josh opened his eyes to find himself sprawled out at home on the living room floor. The house was dark and quiet; even Finnegan, their golden retriever, was sleeping. When Josh stood up to turn on a lamp, he realized his arms and legs didn't hurt any more. He held his breath as he flicked on the lamp and examined them. The skin on his hands and feet was perfect—there was no sign of his burns or any other injuries. A great big smile crossed his face. "I don't believe it. I'm healed."

Will stirred on the floor nearby. Ellen's eyes flickered open as she struggled to wake up.

"Ellen, look!" he exclaimed. "My burns are completely gone. It's as if I never had them in the first place. It's a miracle!"

She jumped to her feet and ran over to him. "You're right," she said, studying his hands. "It's a miracle. God must have healed you."

Tears filled his eyes. "I feel so embarrassed. I really doubted God for a while. What was I thinking?"

"You doubted God?" said Will, sitting up.

Ellen held out her hand to help Will up. He grabbed on and was halfway up when she gasped and let go of him.

"Ouch!" he cried as he landed on the floor. "What did you do that for? That wasn't nice. That hurt!"

"Look at the carpet! Mom's going to be furious!"

Will rolled over and looked at the floor. A light gray imprint of his body had formed on their brand-new carpet.

"Uh-oh," gulped Will. "It must be from the ash."

"I bet you'll be grounded for a month," said Josh.

"So will both of you," said Will, pointing to the spots where Josh and Ellen had been lying. The shape of their bodies was etched on the carpet in ash on either side of his.

"What should we do?" Will wrung his hands as he stared at the mess.

Ellen glanced at the clock as it chimed twelve o'clock. "Let's leave Mom a note. We'll clean it up first thing in the morning."

Josh scrounged around until he found a piece of paper and began writing.

> *Dear Mom,*
>
> *Sorry about the volcanic ash on the floor. We didn't want to vacuum in the middle of the night and wake you up so we'll clean it up in the morning. Don't worry. We think it will come out.*
>
> *Love, Josh, Will, and Ellen*

He carefully placed the paper on the floor beside the mess and then he drew a giant heart in the ash. He took a step back to admire his handiwork and then he added four words in the middle of the heart: "I love my family."

Will and Ellen gave him a big smile. The three of them went upstairs to their bedrooms, leaving a trail of gray footsteps in their wake.

Listen, my son, to your father's instruction
and do not forsake your mother's teaching.
They will be a garland to grace your head
and a chain to adorn your neck.

Proverbs 1:8–9

ESCAPE FROM THE VOLCANO

Life Issue: I want to put God first in my life.
Spiritual Building Block: Honor

THINK ABOUT IT

Escape from the Volcano is based on the fifth commandment: honor your father and mother. In this adventure, Josh didn't understand the commandment; he thought he was smarter than everyone else and continually defied many of the adults he encountered. Remember how he disobeyed the village chief, the priest, and his friend P. L.? His choices got him into a lot of trouble, eventually putting him in serious danger. In this book, Josh is a great example of how *not* to behave.

Many people study the last six of the Ten Commandments as a set because they tell us how we are to get along as people. It's not surprising that God put the commandment about the family first in this group. The family is the center point around which God organized the world. For many of us, our families are the people we know the best. They stay with us for our entire lives.

God began human history by creating a family. After God created Adam, he said, "It is not good for the man to be alone" (Genesis 2:18) and he created Eve. Together, Adam and Eve made the first family. Even the animals were created male and female, and each species made up their own family. After God destroyed the world through the great flood, Noah and his family and each pair of animals were the families that re-created the world (Genesis 7:1–3). God started Israel through Abraham's family, Jesus came to us through Mary and Joseph's family, and the Bible calls the church the "family of God." The family has always had a special place in God's heart.

If you think about the fifth commandment, "Honor your father and mother, so that you may live long in the land the LORD your God is giving you" (Exodus 20:12), you'll notice there are three distinct parts. First, we are commanded to "honor" our parents. It is important for us to do this. Second, there is a promise for the people who honor their parents: They will "live long in the land." Did you know the fifth commandment is the only one with a promise? This commandment is so important to God that he promises to bless with long life if we honor our parents. Third, we are reminded that God is the one who gives the blessing of the land—he is the source of everything.

TALK ABOUT IT

What exactly does it mean to honor your mother and father? If we look at the Bible's teaching, we are told to love our brothers and sisters and neighbors, but our parents are put into a higher category. We are to honor them. Honoring is even greater than loving.

Honoring includes things like choosing to be obedient instead of having your own way, treating your parents with respect, and looking after their needs when they get older because it's the right thing to do. We're not supposed to honor our parents out of a sense of duty but because we love our mom and dad and we're thankful for the good things they've done for us. Our hearts need to be right when we honor our parents.

TRY IT

What are some of the ways you can honor your mom and dad today? Can you say something kind to them? Do your chores with a good attitude? Listen to them respectfully even if you disagree with what they're saying? Your parents have feelings just like you do. When you disobey or speak harshly to them, they hurt too. Treat them the same way you want to be treated.

One of my sons often comes up to me, gives me a big hug, and says, "Mom, what can I help you with today?" This is one of the nicest things he can say to me. Two good things happen when he says this: I feel blessed to be his mom because he's honored me by asking this question, and he pleases God because he's following the fifth commandment. Honoring our parents is a good way to practice honoring God.

COLLECT THEM ALL!

Rescue in the Mayan Jungle
Mystery in the Medieval Castle
Treachery in the Ancient Laboratory
Terror in Hawk's Village

The Word at Work Around the World

A vital part of Cook Communications Ministries is our international outreach, Cook Communications Ministries International (CCMI). Your purchase of this book, and of other books and Christian-growth products from Cook, enables CCMI to provide Bibles and Christian literature to people in more than 150 languages in 65 countries.

Cook Communications Ministries is a not-for-profit, self-supporting organization. Revenues from sales of our books, Bible curricula, and other church and home products not only fund our U.S. ministry, but also fund our CCMI ministry around the world. One hundred percent of donations to CCMI go to our international literature programs.

CCMI reaches out internationally in three ways:

• Our premier International Christian Publishing Institute (ICPI) trains leaders from nationally led publishing houses around the world.

• We provide literature for pastors, evangelists, and Christian workers in their national language.

• We reach people at risk—refugees, AIDS victims, street children, and famine victims—with God's Word.

Word Power, God's Power

Faith Kidz, RiverOak, Honor, Life Journey, Victor, NexGen — every time you purchase a book produced by Cook Communications Ministries, you not only meet a vital personal need in your life or in the life of someone you love, but you're also a part of ministering to José in Colombia, Humberto in Chile, Gousa in India, or Lidiane in Brazil. You help make it possible for a pastor in China, a child in Peru, or a mother in West Africa to enjoy a life-changing book. And because you helped, children and adults around the world are learning God's Word and walking in his ways.

Thank you for your partnership in helping to disciple the world. May God bless you with the power of his Word in your life.

For more information about our international ministries, visit www.ccmi.org.

Additional copies of ESCAPE FROM THE VOLCANO

Date Due

| BRODART, INC. | Cat. No. 23 233 | Printed in U.S.A. |

Equipping Kids for Life